Naughty
Fairy
Tales
from
A to Z

Naughty Fairy Tales from A to Z

Edited by *Alison Tyler*

26 RACY RETOLD FAIRY TALES, FABLES, AND NURSERY RHYMES

A PLUME BOOK

PLUME
Published by the Penguin Group
Penguin Group (USA) Inc., 375 Hudson Street,
New York, New York 10014, U.S.A.
Penguin Books Ltd, 80 Strand, London WC2R 0RL, England
Penguin Books Australia Ltd, 250 Camberwell Road,
Camberwell, Victoria 3124, Australia
Penguin Books Canada Ltd, 10 Alcorn Avenue,
Toronto, Ontario, Canada M4V 3B2
Penguin Books India (P) Ltd, 11 Community Centre, Panchsheel Park,
New Delhi – 110 017, India
Penguin Books (NZ), cnr Airborne and Rosedale Roads,
Albany, Auckland 1310, New Zealand
Penguin Books (South Africa) (Pty) Ltd, 24 Sturdee Avenue,
Rosebank, Johannesburg 2196, South Africa

Penguin Books Ltd, Registered Offices:
80 Strand, London WC2R 0RL, England

Published by Plume, a member of Penguin Group (USA) Inc.
This is an authorized reprint of a hardcover edition published by
Venus Book Club. For information address Venus Book Club,
401 Franklin Avenue, Garden City, New York 11530.

First Plume Printing, September 2004
1   3   5   7   9   10   8   6   4   2

CIP data is available.
ISBN 0-7394-3882-4 (hc.)
ISBN 0-452-28555-0 (pbk.)

Printed in the United States of America

Once upon a time, I kissed a handsome waiter upstairs at a chic Manhattan restaurant while my date thought I was innocently making a phone call. The waiter, who had been softly flirting with me all through dinner, pressed me up against the wall so that I could feel how hard he was, and he wrapped my hair around his fist as he kissed me. I knew exactly what it would be like to fuck him, the ruthless intensity of his thrusts, the way I'd ache all over afterward. We made out until my lips felt bruised, my legs felt weak, and I could hardly remember my date's name when I shakily made my way back downstairs.

—Excerpt from "Once Upon a Time"

For SAM,
my very own handsome prince
from my very own frisky fairy tale.

"I used to be Snow White, but I drifted."

—Mae West

❧ CONTENTS ❧

xii   *Contents*

WHAT THE STORIES ARE BASED ON

⊰ INTRODUCTION ⊱

NCE upon a time, a naughty-minded editor decided to gather together a collection of frisky fairy tales. This sultry, dark-eyed minx of an editor with her cascade of shining black hair and pale complexion quite resembled Snow White herself. While gazing at her reflection in her favorite gilded mirror, she realized that she desperately longed for a group of sexually explicit stories that would entertain and arouse. She yearned to read the type of bedtime stories for grown-ups that would titillate while tantalizing, with delectable descriptions and seriously scrumptious sex acts.

"Mirror, mirror on the wall," the editor whispered. "Who writes the naughtiest stories of them all?"

"You know that full well," the mirror replied shortly.

"Work with me, mirror," the editor cajoled. "I'm desperate for the special type of kinky writing that only the cleverest of authors are capable of delivering."

"If you pitch it, they will write," the mirror replied.

"How true!" the editor thought.

With these words of wisdom, the editor set out to gather her own prized storybook collection. However, although she had an idea as a framework, she let her authors run free with their imaginations. No limits were put on the types of stories that could be submitted. All the editor required was that each story paid homage to the fairy tale genre and that every story would make a reader shiver with waves of naughty anticipation.

Soon the stories appeared magically by e-mail from all over the land. And, oh, was the editor ever satisfied! Authors such as Sage Vivant, M. Christian, Dante Davidson, and Thomas Roche leaped to the X-rated challenge, penning salacious stories so ripe and risqué they made the editor blush a deep rose red as she drank them in.

Now suddenly we're at Happily Ever After—the all-time favorite three words in any story. In fairy tales and fables, this ending is expected and generally involves matrimony. In erotic creations, those words often come after an earth-shattering sexual climax. *This* collection mixes the best of fairy tale fantasy with the very dreamiest kind of extremely dirty erotic concoctions—some authors penned brand-new tales of wonder featuring such interesting creations as sexually ravenous ghosts and magical orgasm-inducing warm summer breezes, while others used well-known stories, Mother Goose rhymes, and fairy tales as their foundation. (Several authors even tackled the same fairy tale, with drastically different results!) But take it from one who knows—the stories in this collection aren't quite what you'll remember from childhood reading hours.

For instance:

Cinderella wears combat boots.

Zoe White lives with seven *whores*.

Wicked sisters occasionally come out on top, sexually speaking.

And Rapunzel's "Tower" is a sex club in San Francisco, where naughty princesses are routinely punished, their glorious long hair pulled and their haughty derrieres paddled to perfection.

Bedtime reading has never been quite so wonderfully naughty before!

Your Editrix,
Alison Tyler
Point Reyes Station, CA
August 2003

Naughty Fairy Tales from A to Z

All McQueen's Men

⊰ BY ALISON TYLER ⊱

N the case of Julissa McQueen, it wasn't Humpty-Dumpty but a relationship that couldn't be put back together. Perhaps, it wasn't much of a relationship to start with, but Julissa had tried for so long to put up with Raymond's innumerable idiosyncracies that she wasn't ready to give up on couplehood. Not without a fight.

Turned out to be a big fight. A mean one, with Raymond cruelly claiming that she'd been obviously unfaithful to him, and Julissa storming out of the couple's penthouse apartment in tears.

"You with your goddamn poker face," he called down the hallway after her. "Finally, showing a little human emotion! Didn't know you had it in you—"

Cliché, she thought as she stalked around the block, the heels of her glossy knee-high black boots click-clacking on the pavement. Such a fucking cliché. He couldn't accept her fiery independence, so he chose to attack her rather than deal with his own insecurities. The thing of it was that she *hadn't* ever cheated. Not on Raymond nor any one of her previous boyfriends. The concept didn't fit her style.

If a connection with a man faded, she ended the relationship before moving onto the next one.

Sure, she might have had a *thought* of cheating—but who didn't? Once or twice when an interesting specimen looked her way, she lost herself in a decadent daydream involving a satisfying situation with someone new. Perhaps while on the subway, or at the grocery store, or out on a morning run. But she'd never actually gone through with it.

Now that Raymond claimed she had—and she was fuming at the false accusation—she thought that maybe she should. Why be blamed for something, be punished for it, really, without experiencing the pleasure of actually screwing someone else?

Someone else named Blake.

And someone else named Sam.

And even someone else named Nelson.

Yes, she had them all lined up in her mind, and as she turned the corner and entered her favorite English bar, "All the King's Horses," there they were, as if they'd been magically positioned there, waiting for her: All McQueen's Men.

In truth, they were her poker buddies. She loved the game, had been a pro for years, but she'd never had much luck playing cards with girls. Ladies didn't seem to put as much thought into the mental warplay of poker. Generally speaking, girls lost interest in their hands and started talking about clothes, or hair, or men. Julissa couldn't stand that. When *she* played cards, she wanted serious adversaries, men who had no qualms about taking her money. She wanted poker faces.

Raymond wasn't into cards. He liked playing the ponies. Or watching football on television. He didn't understand why she felt the need to join her buddies in the smoke-filled private room at the bar, where Nelson, who owned the place, had a weekly game. Raymond was invited, but after going twice, he backed out permanently. Julissa came every week. Or, attended every week. Mentally, she came every once in a while when thinking about what might take place with the three studly guys who joined her at the green felt-flocked table.

Tonight was the night she'd find out.

"There she is," Blake grinned at her, motioning to the others that she'd arrived. "Let the games begin."

Julissa just smiled as she brushed a lock of midnight hair out of her startling cat-shaped eyes, and then followed the trio to the back room. Before anyone could cut the deck of cards this evening, Julissa perched herself on the edge of the table and said, "Let's raise the stakes tonight—"

Sam tilted his head at her as he waited for her to continue.

"What's on your mind?" Nelson wanted to know.

"Strip poker," Blake guessed, patting Julissa on the back with one of his large hands, touching her in an almost buddy style that lingered just a beat too long for someone who wanted to be strictly friends.

"No," she said, shaking her head. Her long, dark hair tickled against her cheeks. "Fuck poker."

"Fuck *poker?*" Sam repeated, shocked. "What do you mean. You don't like playing with us anymore?"

"She's leaving us, boys," Blake said sadly, as if he'd always expected the sad day would eventually come, but he had hoped against hope that it wouldn't arrive so soon.

"Not 'fuck the game,'" she quickly explained, reaching for the deck of cards and shuffling expertly. The cards danced mesmerizingly between her fingers. "But a game played for the stakes of fucking—" Another hesitation. "Fucking me, that is." One final pause, "If you're interested."

She watched the men carefully to see when they would get it. One by one, she saw the moment when they understood what she was saying—and one by one, they nodded in agreement, nodded as if they didn't care if she were pulling their chains, they definitely wanted in. Julissa, herself, wasn't entirely sure of what she was saying. She knew what she needed. Thought about it enough, honestly, to have the scene entirely choreographed from start to finish. Handsome Sam would be in front of her, his faded blue jeans open, cock out, and she would lick from his balls to the tip of his shaft as Blake slid her soft skirt up to her hips and lowered her panties. Tonight, she had on a pair of pale lilac-colored ones made of lace-trimmed silk.

She wanted Nelson between her legs, lapping fiercely her pussy while Blake prepared her to receive his cock from behind, back-door style. And by back door, she really meant that she wanted Blake to take her ass. Raymond wouldn't do that with her. Not that he hadn't ass-fucked a girl before, because he had and she knew it. They'd teased each other with one of those "what have you done" conversations early on in their relationship, in the playful stage before they'd gotten serious. So yeah, she knew he'd ass-fucked a French girl in New York one summer. But he didn't do it that way with Julissa, and for some reason with him refusing, that only made her want to go that route even more.

So, she saw it all, had fantasized so often she felt as if she'd seen the image in a dirty movie, but that didn't mean it was going to happen. The boys had to win first, and winning wouldn't be easy. Julissa was an ace at poker. Nobody ever knew exactly what she was thinking.

"Really?" Sam asked now, and Julissa realized that her poker face was already in place. The guys truly didn't know whether or not she was putting them on.

"Really," Julissa said, dealing out the first hand.

"And Raymond?" Blake asked.

"Fuck Raymond," Julissa spat. It was clear to all of them that "fuck Raymond" was an entirely different statement from "fuck poker," and none of the men commented further. They sat down, eyeing each other carefully, and lifted their cards.

Even though she wanted this fantasy to come true more than anything else she'd ever wanted, Julissa couldn't lose on purpose. That wouldn't be right. But the guys turned out to want the evening's culmination even more than she did. For the first time ever, they created a three-man team, and they fought hard, all of them, to beat her down. Which they did. As soon as she started to lose, Julissa felt that the inevitable was happening. She couldn't draw the cards she needed, couldn't fake the boys out with any of her standard moves. Slowly, she began to accept that her fantasy was going to come true, and that made the cards shake in her hands.

"Nervous," Sam asked, reaching out to stroke her knee gently under the table.

"No," she said, folding her final hand, and she realized as she said the word that she wasn't nervous at all. She was excited, desperately wet, and ready to get started. "Let me tell you how it's going to be—"

They listened carefully to her precise instructions, and then they took their positions around her. Sam was in front, as he had to be, with his jeans splayed open, awaiting the first gentle lick of her tongue on his naked cock. He looked down at her in total awe, as she parted her full berry-slicked lips and let him in. And just as she surrounded Sam's cock with her open mouth, Nelson lowered her panties and pressed his face against her pussy.

"Oh—" Julissa murmured, her mouth full of Sam. "Oh, yes."

Blake didn't jump in right away. He watched the action for several moments before wetting his fingers and tracing them around Julissa's rear hole. He wanted her nice and wet before he plunged, and he wanted a signal from her that this was really what she needed.

Nelson continued to suckle on her clit, and Julissa, bent forward, had her mouth so full of Sam's cock that she couldn't talk at all. But she waggled her lovely ass a little, left and then right, to let Blake know that she was ready. He parted her cheeks wider and then pressed the head of his cock at her asshole. He waited a moment, and then slid in a little bit deeper. Julissa moaned ferociously around Sam's cock, and Sam picked up the pace, sliding back and forth between her lips at a rapid rhythm. Julissa couldn't get enough of him. She swallowed forcefully, and then reached forward to cradle his balls as she continued to work him. She was driven on by the pace of Nelson between her legs and Blake fucking her smoothly from behind. Being taken back there was as exciting as she'd dreamed about. The fact that Raymond had been denying her so long made the pleasure even greater.

The foursome were so self-contained that not one of them heard the knock on the private door, and none noticed the intrusion until they heard a sharp intake of breath, followed by a "What the fuck is going on back here!"

Then Blake looked over his shoulder, raised his eyebrows, and simply shrugged. He was too close to coming to stop at this point. Sam didn't even bother with that much of a response, paying attention instead to the lovely Julissa, gently cradling her head as she sucked him to the root, swallowing every last drop. From his position, Nelson couldn't really see Raymond very clearly, but he knew the man was there. Being watched had always thrilled Nelson, and he put one hand on his own bulging crotch as he continued to lick on Julissa's pulsing clit. He was going to come at the moment she did, and that made his entire body feel alive with impending ecstasy.

As for Julissa, as she glanced over at Raymond's face, she felt a wave of satisfaction beat through her—in the back room of "All the King's Horses," and in the midst of all McQueen's men, it was obvious that this was one relationship that would never be put back together again.

But some stories are like that—for Julissa, it didn't make her evening's ending any less happy.

Bells on Her Toes

⊰ BY M. CHRISTIAN ⊱

JASMINE died two years ago. She showed up three weeks ago. Should have expected it, knowing Jasmine as well as I did.

I didn't know she was back, not really, for almost a week. Stomping around my little Long Beach bungalow, the one she had called my shell, I caught glimpses of faint reds, gold, of the hazy glow of sunlight through baggy tie-dyes, and of God's Eyes turning in the windows. They were just there enough so I knew I saw something, but was always a part, always a fragment of that something. Same with smells: incense, patchouli oil, pot, cheap wine, and that simple lemon perfume. Same with sounds, walking from the little kitchenette into the living room I would catch the slap of leather sandals on the hardwood floors, the opening clap of "Stairway," and that tiny sound, that special sound that would always mean bells on toes. Jasmine.

She had outlasted the ghost of the sixties by a few years, Jasmine had. Even though she'd been born in '71, she was a spirit of the Merry Pranksters, of Airplane, of the Summer of Love, acid, pot, Fat Freddy's Cat, the Stones, and tie-dyes.

It wasn't easy being a flower child in the age of the World Wide Web, ecstasy, coke, NIN, Courtney Love, and body piercings, but Jasmine pulled it off. She drifted with a smile on her face, and those fucking bells on her toes, through life—hitching rides with only good people, taking only the best drugs, being friends with only good people. She was a ghost of the sixties, a spirit of the Haight and the Diggers.

Now she was just a spirit.

I never could figure out how she could exist. She was fascinating in the same way a Mary Keene painting (admit it, you've seen them—big-eyed children) can be: innocence distilled to the point of being surreal. Jasmine could hitchhike with Jeffrey Dahmer and get out alive, and with some money to help her on her way. Deep down, though, I knew her luck couldn't last. Whatever is out there hates the lucky and the innocent.

If there was a sin in Jasmine, in her perfect fortune, this unblinking good luck, it was that it didn't leave much room for depth or brains. Jasmine was a spirit who walked slowly through life, letting it bump her this way and that. Never ask her to meet you anywhere, never make plans around her. Jasmine was pot and incense and a soft, warm body that fit so comfortably in your arms, but she wasn't someone you could count on. No one who knew her said it, but we all knew it was true—and having her turn up two years after we all put her to rest in the Long Beach Municipal Cemetery proved it.

She was late for her own funeral.

I can't really remember the first time I met Jasmine. Maybe it was that party to celebrate Rosie getting her first gig at the Red Room. Maybe it was that picnic that Robert and Steve threw down at the remains of the old Pike. Maybe she had just shown up on my doorstep like she always seemed to, jingling her tiny silver bells and lazily sweeping her tie-dyed skirt back and forth. No place to sleep that night and Roger Corn was always up, awake, and willing to take her in.

God knew what we had in common, save we . . . fit somehow. We didn't talk music (Airplane! NIN! Joplin! Love!) or books (Kesey! Coupland!) or anything else for that matter (You're always so damned happy! What do you have to feel sad about?), we just fucked and played and took our respective drugs (coffee and weed! H and pot!). A spirit of the '60s and one hack writer making his bread and butter writing porn, *True Detective Stories*, and articles on how to get your cat to use the toilet. We just seemed to go together somehow. We tolerated each other because we liked to fuck and kiss each other. Relationships can be based on worse things.

When I got that call, Rosie so calm and collected, I was sort of ready for it. Jasmine always did what you expected her to, if you understood her, so when the phone rang and Rosie said that Jasmine had "passed on," I knew almost exactly how, where, and why.

The funeral was sparse and sad for the little spirit just the four of us. We had all pitched in to get the coffin. It was a colorful affair, you had to give it that: Rosie in a gaudy color blast of a red sequined gown and boa, Robert in his own retro seventies platforms and polyester, Steve with his beads and a (where the fuck did he score that?) Nehru jacket. I wore something aside from black. It was hard to find, but I managed to score a brilliant red shirt from a friend of mine. In many cultures, red is the color for the dead.

Two years later she was paying me a visit.

The first time I realized that something was going on I was scared shitless. I was washing my coffee cup (my lucky one), high a wee bit from this shitty Mexican that Rosie had scored for me, and I felt someone behind me, but I shrugged it off. Then the someone put their arms around my waist and hugged me. I screamed, dropped my cup (*Java Is the Spirit of Creativity*) into shards of ceramic, jumped into my Docs and ran over to Steve and Robert's.

You'd think that OD'ing on H in Rosie's apartment would be enough to keep a girlfriend down.

After a day or so Rosie had convinced me that it was just lack of sleep, too many sips from my favorite mug, and a sudden flash of missing Jasmine. Rosie said she felt her own late ex touch her sometimes—when she was in just the right mood. Of course there are differences between a dyke who'd gone off a bridge on her Harley and Jasmine the flower child overdoing the nostalgia just a bit.

Back in my place I kept seeing those flashes of Jasmine's colors, smelling her smell, and hearing her bells. And sometimes, just before drifting off at three A.M. I'd feel her body warmth—just the heat of her at first, you understand, slip into bed with me.

Then, about two weeks after that first touch in the kitchen, I was coming from the living room into the kitchen, empty new mug in hand (*Coffee Is the Last Refuge of the Sleepy*), straight for my Saint Coffee machine, and there she was: sandals, tie-dyed drawstring pants, simple white cotton shirt, scarf tied over her head. She was just there, at the kitchen counter, reading the paper, as I'd seen her a million times: joint burning in one hand, twirling a few strands of her blonde hair in the other, chewing her lips at some newspaper headline or another and—while she'd never actually said it—you could still hear her thoughts clear and distinct: *Why don't people get along?* Like she had on many mornings, as she had countless times.

And there she was again, after two years cold in the ground.

Then she wasn't. She was there for about as much time as it takes to blink and think, for a panicked second, *Is that really her?*

That was the first time. There were quickly others.

Jasmine liked to get in the bathtub with me when I was practicing my Death Trance Meditations. I sit in warm water with the lights off and think about myself in terms of flesh, blood, bone, hair, and where all those pieces could end up, say, in a million years. You can get into some profound thoughts, laying in the dark, in the water, like that. And it can really mess with your head when the door would crash open and this demented hippie chick, all bounce and giggle, would come storming in jingling her tiny silver bells to pull off her balloon pants and squat herself down on the john to take a piss. We used to fight about it, especially when I didn't even know she was in the house. You can imagine the shock she made after she was dead.

Mornings were Jasmine's favorite time of day. If I'd let her she would go on and on about the opening of the day, with the accompaniment of birds singing and the soft applause of butterflies. She would wax cliché about the possibilities "dawning" (and giggling at the pun) with the new day and wonder how many adventures she'd have by sunset.

I am a Creature of the Night. I run from the burning rays of the sun and seek solstice in the cool darkness of my shell. But, still, I would always get up on a cheery blast furnace of a morning and be happy as a clam—especially when Jasmine treated me to one of her early-bird special blowjobs. She liked that word, "blowjob"—said it sounded cute. And, boy, was Jasmine skilled in its performance. Just the right amount of tongue, suction, lips, wet, dry, hands. She used to wake me up with soft kisses along my leg to let me know she was there and what she was up to. Then the kisses would run up to my stomach. A hand carefully placed over my cock and balls would warm them and add some sensation. When her mouth did finally touch my cock, it was after those soft, soft hands had stroked, teased, tickled, and coaxed me into a painfully intense hard-on. Then the mouth. Then the real ride.

Mornings haven't been the same since she died. The sun must be a little brighter, stronger now. But then that one morning came. I was sleeping off my usual late-night writing stint (with a celebration of a new one finished: *I Was a Teenage Trailer-Park Slut*) when I got this amazing hard-on. I was so zonked that I really can't tell you if it was because of Jasmine or just because I was remembering my past with her, but there it was: long (no brag, but seven inches), strong, and mighty. It was a mechanic's cock, a soldier's cock, a fuckin' basketball player's cock. I was proud of my cock, pleased with it that morning. With a hard-on like that, even hack writers can go out and become president (if you know the right people).

Then Jasmine started to work on it. Dear dead Jasmine. Maybe because of my half-zonked condition, maybe because I just missed those lips, that throat, but I didn't do what I should have done: run screaming into that intense morning. But I didn't, and dear dead Jasmine started to really get down and suck at my cock.

Death did not diminish her knowledge of blowjobs, it seemed. She was all of Jasmine rolled into that one cocksucking. I could, in fact, squint and see her as I had seen her on all those mornings: her firm, slightly heavy body folded over, her face concentrating at my cock, with her right hand between her legs as she humped herself along with her sucking.

God, I could feel every inch of Jasmine—even if I couldn't see her. I could feel her tongue playing with the ridges and corona of my head, I could feel her lips play over my skin and veins, I could feel her throat—hot and firm— as I grazed it during her sucking. When I came, it was so good it hurt real bad, and my come shot into an invisible mouth and vanished into ectoplasmic nothingness just as real live Jasmine had liked to swallow it.

Other people would have run—to their pastors, to the cops, to some science guys with a gizmo to exorcise the latent spectral energies, or to their priests (who would rattle their beads and speak some Latin). But most folks don't consider themselves a Child of the Night, groove on gloom, or hate any color save pitch black. Besides, Jasmine had been a sweet girl (tinkle, tinkle) and one motherfuckin' hot lay

The fact that she was dead and haunting me didn't really seem to bother me at the time.

Jasmine was great for surprises. She liked to catch you unawares and get caught unawares herself. I can't remember how many times I "caught" Jasmine in the living room, or on the toilet, in my bed, rubbing one of her little, soft fingers up and down on her little moist slit. She was like a little kid in that, her body and other people's used to give her so much pleasure. Death didn't even slow her down.

Listening to the newest Lycia CD, all moan, cemeteries, statues, clouds, rain, and mourners, I would get the strong impression of flowers, macramé, pot, and the distinct sound of the tiny silver bells on toes jingling merrily away and look next to me to see Jasmine, half there and half not, not quite developed, not quite visible, legs spread wide, fingers gently rubbing up and down on her gumdrop-sized clit.

She became, over those weeks, to be more and more in my life. More so than she had when she was alive. Flesh-and-blood Jasmine used to come over maybe, tops, three times a week. Then I wouldn't see her for months. Once a year passed before I walked in to see her dancing, naked, in my living room, the air thick with Mexican greenbud. But now that she had passed on, time seemed different to her. I would expect to see or feel this spirit of Morrison, of Cream, of Sergeant Pepper at least once a day. Dancing in the living room, reading the Sunday paper in the kitchen, masturbating on the toilet, spooning with me in bed.

Bad? No, not at all. I felt special that of all the people she had lived with, had fucked, had fought with, this one hack writer living in a cheap-ass bungalow in Long Beach was the one she wanted to spend eternity with.

But there started to be other times, too. I would walk from the kitchen into the living room, coffee cup in hand, straight for my Macintosh with visions of *Truck-Stop Bimbos* running through my head like a pneumatic chorus line, and I would see her, standing by the window looking at something only the ghostly Jasmine could see. What bothered me more than anything was that Jasmine, alive, never really had an interest in the traffic on Oleander Street. Jasmine wasn't just an echo drilled into me and my cheap-ass stucco walls. Something of the real Jasmine was here with the spectral one. Something that was missing something.

It became pretty obvious when she started to get distracted by things. Right in the middle of one hot and nasty morning blowjob, her ghost would stop right in the middle (*coitus spectoralus*) and I would get the definite impression that she was looking out that window again like she was trying to remember something that she had forgotten.

Rosie, my only expert on dead relations coming back to cop a feel, got real quiet as she poured my Darjeeling tea, then said: "When Bolo left this world—" Rosie's ex who tried to jump her Harley from the Queen Mary to Catalina "—she came back to visit me a couple of times. It was like she just wanted to say good-bye in a way she couldn't when she was living. When she had done that, she faded away."

"Yeah, but I don't get the vibe that Jas is here for a reason. It's like she just sort of moved back in."

Rosie stirred her tea with a chiming that reminded me way too much of Jasmine's tiny silver bells. "I got the impression from Bolo that she knew where she was going and that she was just stopping by. Remember, we are dealing with Jasmine, here. She could have gotten lost."

Great, a girl who could get lost in a Safeway had taken the wrong turn between death and the afterlife and was now trapped in my house.

It got worse soon after. The sex was still there, but now it was . . . sad. The one thing the flesh-and-blood Jasmine wasn't was sad. The best way to get rid of her, in fact, was to get depressed: she'd vanish like pot smoke to find someone more cheerful. I've always had a hard time putting on a happy face, the one reason why Jasmine and I never stayed together for too long. Now, though, it looked like she was stuck in my dark little bungalow. Trapped. And it was making her sad. It wasn't something she was used to, getting sad, and it was hitting her hard.

I heard her cry one day. I was hard at work on something for a porno mag when I heard this weird sound. A sort of choking, wet sound. I hadn't heard it before. I found her next to my bed, curled into a partially invisible fetal position. Jasmine was crying. It was that heaving, nauseous kind of crying, the kind you do when you're lost and know you can never find your way back.

I'm not a very altruistic kinda guy. I don't really know where it comes from, or doesn't: I just really don't give a flying fuck for a lot of folks. Yeah, I'll take Steve to the hospital when his T cells are low, or hold Rosie when she thinks too much of Bolo, but I don't really see those things are being good. Good is, like, helping fucking orphans or something, or giving change to the crackhead who hangs out, or passes out, at the Laundromat. I don't have that kind of temperament.

I really didn't care that much about Jasmine. Yeah, I'd bail her out when she got busted for forgetting her purse and eating up a storm at some diner. Yeah, I'd give her whatever I had in my checking account when she really needed it. Yeah, I'd always let her in, no matter what was going on in my life. But she was just a pal, and a really good lay. I honestly didn't think of her in any other terms.

But then she was dead, and crying in my bedroom.

I could guess the cause. Bolo was a dyke who always knew where she was going and exactly how to get there.

She was an iron-plated mean mother who knew what the score was—despite her profound depressions and mood swings. Jasmine was flowers and pot and the Beatles. She could get lost walking from the bathroom into the bedroom.

It wasn't all that hard, once I made the decision to do it. One phone call, to Rosie. Then into the bathroom.

I hadn't done my Death Trance since she had manifested herself those two weeks ago. It was just too much of a temptation for her, and the shock of her walking in had been way too much when she was flesh and blood. Since she was a ghost—well, I don't really want to see if I'm cardiac prone.

Had trouble sleeping a few years back. I was lucky enough to have health insurance at the time, so I was able to see a doc who could actually give me pills. I had only taken one—the fuckers were so strong that I stopped taking them and simply started staying up late.

I took five and lay down in the warm water.

We are nothing but matter. We are nothing but the flesh that hangs on our bones, the blood that gushes through our meat. We are animals that have learned to walk upright, that have trained themselves to use the next best thing to fishing with termites with a stick: the nuclear bomb.

I didn't have to think long. About the time I was drawling analogies between Sartre and seals that know how to play "Lady of Spain" on car horns, I was interrupted by a tiny sound, the sound of cheap Mexican toe rings chiming their tinny, cheap tones: the tinkling of tiny silver bells. Then the sound of Jasmine pissing into the toilet.

But this time it didn't sound mischievous; it sounded sad.

The pills had started to take effect, I braced my feet

against the tub so I wouldn't drown and whispered, as loud as I could (which was just loud enough for the dead to hear), "Follow me."

I don't know what she saw, but I started to hallucinate pretty badly. Either the pills, or I had really started to fade, myself—I don't know. I was in the kitchen, full and real and solid, looking out my window. The sun was bright, so bright that I had to close my eyes against the brightness—but for some reason it reached right through my eyelids and right into my brain. I realized then that it couldn't be the sun—for at least the obvious reason that sun never came in that window, anyway.

No tunnel, no saints (or sinners, either), just that bright light. I felt myself start to come apart, like the flesh I had always talked about, thought about in my trances, was starting to unravel and decompose around me, leaving just a lightweight fragment of Roger Corn left. It wasn't a pull or an enticement, it was just a direction that I was walking myself to.

Jasmine. Somewhere I thought that, and reached back into my apartment for her, but I couldn't seem to find her. I looked in the bathroom (I looked so silly laying there in the tub, mouth hanging open), the living room, all the closets, the kitchen . . . everywhere. No Jasmine. Not even her ghost.

Then that sound. Her sound. Cheap bells on her toes and a smile on her face. I found her masturbating in the bedroom, chubby legs wide and open, finger dancing on her clit. Typical. I smiled and took her hand and pulled her toward me, into me—

—and then pushed her away, into the brightness.

The cops and firemen busted down my bathroom door

about that time. I don't remember much after save the sound of their tools smashing my interior door to cheap splinters. Rosie had come through, with perfect timing.

No repercussions, no real ones at any rate: what's another botched suicide, after all. At least I had accomplished something with this one: a spectral repercussion.

She's gone. You'd expect that. Gone wherever magical little Deadheads go when they OD. She's with Janis now, with Morrison and Lennon—in a place where the seventies never happened and where everyone gets along.

And, yeah, I hear those damned happy bells now and again.

Clever Jack

⊰ BY TYLER MORGAN ⊱

ACK wasn't scared of much. Not the action of sliding into someone else's pad late at night. Not the thought of being arrested and the possible inconvenience and probable embarrassment that might mean. But that didn't mean he was entirely fearless. Everyone has their limits—and Jack knew his.

He thought about the man who'd clued him into this score, a strange whacked-out dude in a patched-up tuxedo, who had asked Jack to trade him his café au lait for a packet of dried bean chili. Mad stuff. Jack hadn't even wanted to pause and have a conversation based on what was clearly a matter of total insanity, but the man had been insistent.

"Come on, I know you, Jack," the man had said, "I understand you up here." He'd tapped Jack's temple lightly. "You want to make the big leagues, don't you? I have a deal for you," and he'd hustled Jack down a nearby alley, sipping from Jack's drink before he could stop him, and then spelling out the plans to hit a huge château in the ritzy part of town. One that Jack was personally tied to.

Now, as Jack snuck through the darkened mansion, he

breathed slowly and calmly, making almost no noise at all. He was after a special sort of treasure—an heirloom known as "the Golden Harp." There was already a buyer waiting for this priceless piece, and snatching it would mean that Jack's days of thievery were over.

And this concept actually was what scared him the most.

He lived for adrenaline. The rush of going where he was unwanted. The thrill of getting away without anyone being the wiser. In his day-to-day dealings, nobody would ever have guessed his true identity. He was a strong silent type, but a good guy. Almost a Boy Scout in his heroic stature. The way he kept himself at that high moral level was by being devious after dark. No longer would he need to. Could he give it up? He wasn't entirely sure.

The thing was that *she* wanted him to. Dana. She was both the reason he was in this house and the reason he'd never sneak into another one. Knowing that filled Jack with a bittersweet sensation. Part sadness. Part satisfaction. He reached the heavy metal safe without a problem and entered the code he'd memorized by heart. Within the safe lay the treasure, and Jack's large black-gloved hand gently closed around the diamond-encrusted golden pin. How something so small could be worth so much never ceased to amaze him. Now wasn't the time to have those thoughts. He quickly closed the safe and retraced his steps, hurrying to escape undetected.

And that's when he heard the footsteps.

Jack slammed himself against one wall, holding his breath. The mansion was supposed to be empty. But "supposed to" wasn't going to save him now. His heart raced, his body hummed. The door opened, and in a shaft of white-gold light he saw a tall, lean silhouette. Would she pass by? Would she turn on the light?

She entered the room slowly and then flicked on the overhead chandelier. Here was the lady of the house. Jack found himself looking her over. The woman was built like a runway model, tall and fine-boned, with long dark hair brushed severely off her face, and eyes the inky black color of obsidian. Her cheeks were always flushed, even though she never wore blush, and she had a glow about her that sometimes made Jack pause, forgetting whatever he was thinking about saying, doing. She captivated him, both with her beauty and the fact that there was something solid about her, even with her delicate structure. She had on leather tonight, and long knee-length boots that he knew cost several thousands of dollars, and she moved with a grace that made Jack think of an animal. Panther. Lioness. Some big female cat.

"Jack," she said, shaking her head in a sad way. "You fell for his line, did you?"

"I'm sorry," he said.

Her dark eyes flashed at him. "No, you're not. You could be, though. I could make you sorry."

"What do you mean?" he asked, watching as she took the harp and set it down on the table.

"You like the thrill," she said, "but I don't want to lose you. These months apart have taught me that. I can give you other sorts of thrills, if you'll let me. A trade-off, if you will."

Jack took a deep breath and then nodded. He wasn't precisely sure what he was agreeing to, but whatever this woman wanted of him, he would give.

"Thought you knew better," she said, reaching for his belt and deftly undoing the silver metal buckle.

"Couldn't stay away," he said, agreeing with her.

"But listening to that old freak show?" she was talking about her former butler, a man Jack knew well enough from when he and Dana had dated. "He was the one who coerced you into coming, right?"

"Not 'coerced,'" Jack said softly, watching her every move. "He reminded me of what I was missing."

"My jewelry?"

"You know that's not why I'm here."

"You're right," Dana said, pulling him toward her and kissing his mouth with a hot intensity that he remembered from all of their previous cinematic-style clinches together. He felt himself melt into her kiss. "I know exactly why you're here, bad boy," she said when they parted. "So get over to that couch and wait for it."

He did as she commanded, moving quickly, knowing that Dana would be able to punish him thoroughly without making him come. Knowing that she'd save the greatest pleasure for later, heating him up until he reached fever point, keeping him on the brink until long after he paid her with pain. Jack's goal always was to take it, to prove that he could withstand whatever she had to give. He couldn't get enough of the rush that came with surrendering for this woman.

She was a fine dominant, his girl. She knew how to take control. How odd that he lived for being in control of himself—when on a spree, when planning a theft—but in bed, he needed to give up everything. Needed to surrender his very soul to his mate. Dana was the only woman who ever fully understood that and accepted the fact as if nothing could be more natural. She was his match. To her, administering a strict whipping before fucking him was the most basic and greatly anticipated pleasure on earth.

That's what she planned on doing now, but she started slowly, using his own belt to lightly tan his ass. She let the leather fall on him, not striking yet, only tempting him with the gentle weight of the hide on his own hide. Each clap against his skin reminded him of a different night with her, sometimes bound to her bed, other times cuffed to a chair, occasionally forced to take the brunt of her sadistic nature without any ties at all.

Why they'd ever split, he couldn't fathom now. Yeah, he knew the reasons. Knew that they'd sounded fine, on paper, anyway. But he and Dana were meant for each other. They wouldn't part again. *That* he was sure of.

"See if you can make it through twenty tonight without coming all over my expensive leather couch, all right?" Dana whispered as she pushed his soft brown hair out of his eyes. "Clever Jack, can you do that? Do you think you can do that for me?"

"Anything you want, Dana," Jack murmured, feeling her fingers trace along his naked skin. "Anything you want."

Ducks to Swans

—☙ BY MIA UNDERWOOD ❧—

ELLY was one of the swans. Every school has several, preening peahens who like to strut their stuff. But Kelly was the queen, one of those nymphets blessed from the beginning with the perfect bodies and perfect smiles. The kind who blossom magically from cute kid to curvaceous woman without the awkward puberty stage the majority of us suffer through.

I wasn't so lucky, and Kelly let me know that every day for four years. She had it for me, putting me down whenever she could from the first day of high school on through graduation. She wasn't cruel only to me, but to most every girl in the school who didn't make it on the cheerleading squad (or who didn't bother to try out).

The typical ugly duckling, I had no idea that someday I might actually join the ranks of the white-feathered ones. Or, at the very least, a condor, an egret, some delicately beautiful creation that would make bird-watchers (and girl-watchers) stop and take notice. My legs grew before the rest of me developed, so I was extra tall for a freshman. I didn't get over being gangly until my senior year in college.

Then, although it wasn't overnight, I underwent a transformation. My body was at its peak—I'd joined the track team and all those afternoon practices paid off. My long legs were toned and well muscled. My ass was . . . well, what an ass lays awake at night and dreams about being.

I found that sense of peace that is rare and sought after. I'd always liked who I was inside. Now, I seriously liked who I was outside. After that, things only continued to get better.

I'd never have thought to attend a stupid reunion, but my best girlfriend urged me to. "Go show them what you've become," she insisted. "Do it for closure." I'd like to say that's why I went, but it wasn't. Kelly had been on my mind lately, haunting me with her fantasy images. Taunting me.

I bought a black, slinky dress, paid more than I ever had before to get my hair cut and styled, did an expert job with my makeup, and went.

It's true what they say about reunions. Many pretty people get ugly, and many ugly people get pretty. I looked around the rented hotel meeting room and attempted to place names with remembered faces. When Kelly walked up to me, I don't really know which one of us was more surprised.

"You've changed," she said.

I looked her over. She, of all the once-pretty ones, had *stayed* pretty. She looked dynamic in a purple velvet dress that showed off her still-stunning figure. I closed my eyes and thought back to all the times she'd referred to me as a giraffe, taking to calling me that in public so that other people latched onto it and used it as my nickname.

"Not so giraffelike," I said, finally.

She tilted her head at me in that cute, cheerleader way, then said, "Sometimes kids can be cruel . . . especially when they're jealous."

I waited for her to continue.

"You always had it together. You got good grades, and you had those legs . . ." she looked me up and down, "*have* those legs," she corrected herself, then surprised me even more by placing her hand on my waist and pulling me closer to her.

"I've wanted to see them undressed for ever so long."

"Have you?" I asked, enjoying my newfound role of the desired. She nodded, and I smiled and followed her out of the room and to the elevators. We rode in silence to her room, and, once we were through the front door, barely made it to her bed. I undressed quickly, while she watched, but when I got to my garters she stopped me. "Leave those," she said, "please."

The sex was incredible. Making love to a cheerleader had been a fantasy of mine for far too long, and despite the ten years since graduation, Kelly still knew how to make the audience (of one, this time) take notice.

She didn't want to fuck, at first. She stroked my legs through the sheer stockings, then got on her knees at the edge of the bed and made love to each one of my pearl-polished toes through my sparkling stockings, suckling on them, teasing them. It was a new sensation to me, and I have to admit the action got me extremely wet. Watching that perfect mouth of hers open up to take in my slender digits made me wetter than I'd ever been. I might have come from her foot worship alone, but she climbed onto the bed and began sucking on my nipples. She definitely had an oral fixation, placing her mouth on anything that protruded: my tits, my toes, my clit when it got so hot and wet that it stood up away from its covering hood.

That was the best, watching the queen of my high school part my thighs and go hungrily for my cunt. She didn't care about her mussed hair, her smeared lipstick, the slick gloss of my juices on her chin. She was suddenly just a woman, a lover, a true human being. And as she bowed to the altar of my body, I was suddenly the same, grabbing her and moving her into a sixty-nine, so that I could bestow the same gifts to her own wet pussy with my ravenous mouth. She tasted sweet, a candy-dream treat.

There were candid shots of Kelly throughout our high school yearbook. Her looking cute and posing for the camera . . . what the photographer would have given to have the shots I have immortalized in my mind.

Earthly Delights

By FLORENCE HOARD

RISSY was not so much locked in the castle as she was unprepared to be anywhere else. The castle sat quite fixedly on the enormous Precipice of Paradise overlooking the Sea of Tranquillity. Lining the slopes of the precipice and encircling the sea was the dense, rich foliage of the Forest of Earthly Delights. A sliver of beach separated the sea from the forest.

Prissy had a vague but pleasant memory of once touching that sand, of playing near the lapping waves. It must have been while her parents were still alive, before she was three years old. In the seventeen years since, she would look out from the castle tower fondly, with only a vague twinge of longing, at the modest beach.

Do not misunderstand, reader. Prissy's life was a happy one, both before and after her parents' deaths. The castle was full of kind servants, several of whom had children, and she lived among aunts, uncles, and cousins. The Precipice of Paradise was most aptly named.

Her primary ward and protector, if any government official had ever been interested enough to inquire, was her

Uncle Mikhail, the brother of her father. He'd not had any daughters of his own, and so when the beautiful blonde child was suddenly deprived of her parents, he adopted her with an unwavering commitment to ensure her welfare and safety.

She'd been educated, clothed, fed, entertained, and nurtured exclusively on the Precipice of Paradise. Everything she needed had always been within castle walls.

Until the day the dove visited.

It was an afternoon where the sunshine fired the castle walls' brilliance and the air would surely crackle if it were any clearer. Had she tried, she was certain she could touch the sky's blueness. The arrival of the dove on Prissy's parapet perch seemed quite natural. She extended her hand to invite the dove to rest on her fingers. The dove hopped to her hand happily.

"What have we here?" Prissy asked, noticing a small, folded paper stuck under its wing. She pulled it gently from the white plumage. She unfolded the paper and discovered a message inside.

The beach withers from loneliness, awaiting your return.

She stared at the words and read them again. And again. She read them aloud to the dove, as if seeking an explanation from the messenger. The bird merely cocked its head and cooed.

The message so confused her that she retreated inside, closing the heavy door between her room and the drum tower. She left the dove wondering at her sudden departure.

Of course, she knew that a beach could not write a letter, let alone feel lonely. Someone had to be down there, on that beautiful stretch of sand, waiting for her. For seventeen years? Oh, this was most vexing!

She did not join the family for dinner that evening, leaving word with her lady-in-waiting of a sudden illness. The news prompted an immediate visit from Uncle Mikhail.

She would not admit him. Through her door, she implied she suffered from some mysterious feminine malady, knowing he would retreat out of quiet respect. In minutes, he returned to the dinner table, leaving her to lament in silence.

Should she have told him of the note? No, he would dismiss it, not wanting to upset her. She did not wish for protection now, only the truth.

Fretting to the point of exhaustion, she finally stored the note in her small, secret treasure box hidden beneath her underclothes in her dresser drawer, and retired to her bed.

She slept fitfully. Finally, she awoke, consumed by a restless inner fire that demanded she rise. Her room felt small, and she burned with claustrophobic panic. She threw back her fine linens and rushed toward the door she had closed so firmly that afternoon.

Flinging the great door wide open, an unseasonably strong wind rushed inside, sending her diaphanous gown billowing around her body. But the zealous breeze did not cool her as it should have. Instead, it caressed and licked at her body, insistently, provocatively. It was nearly the temperature of her own skin, dancing around her, stroking her. She closed her eyes, reached up and grabbed her wavy hair at its roots. She felt she should not succumb to the vague hungers the wind inspired. The hungers were unfamiliar. They made her want to touch herself.

She walked to the edge of the tower, inhaling in quick, shallow breaths. How she wanted to see the beach! But the evening fog sat heavily upon the sea and even obscured much of the forest.

Something or someone compelled her, though; of that she was certain. The pull was matched only by the wanton strokes of the wind over her body.

Her temperature rose and hot moisture formed between her legs. Her nipples had grown hard. As the breeze whipped her gown against them, the stimulation overwhelmed her. In response, she slipped the straps over her shoulders and let the bodice fall and gather at her waist. She stood in the foggy night with naked breasts turned toward the moonlight. The breeze seemed to kiss her. Still, she struggled to stay in control.

She opened her legs to let the breeze tickle her thighs and lick at the damp thatch of hair at their apex. Her knees weakened and her head spun. The fever burned relentlessly.

"Prissy," came a subtle whisper. She felt the breath of it more than she heard the sound. Hands took gentle hold of her breasts, squeezing and kneading, making her moan. She looked down and saw the hands were her own, but the realization did not halt her movements. Rather, the sight of her breasts worked by her own hands excited her. The wind repeated her name and snaked a thin line from her stomach past her sternum and up her chest and neck, like a lover's curious tongue.

A new sensation flooded her private regions. Her labia were full and wet with slick juice of her own making. Was it just the wind so expertly exploring her secret folds? She threw her head back and moaned in surrender. The air then wriggled further, attacking her tiny but engorged love button with furious, targeted gusts.

The fire inside her was now centered between her legs. Her pulse emanated from her wet nexus, and she feared she would explode from her skin. The release that came made her call out and lose her balance. It wracked her with delicious waves of pleasure that brought tears to her eyes.

She lay crumpled atop the tower, her limbs loose and her mind empty. Such pleasure! The wind ceased and the usual, cool night air enveloped her. What kind of storm had just passed through? Or was she dreaming? When she felt the evening chill her, she rose slowly and returned to bed, too distracted to close the door behind her. She slept soundly and undisturbed, and awoke with a serenity that made her grin.

But as she lay there with daybreak streaming into her room, her fears slowly returned. Was last night's activity somehow related to the note? Should she speak of either event to her uncle? She remembered her hands clutching her breasts and the intensity of her pleasure. Instinctively, she knew she must keep her story to herself.

The dove she'd met the day before swooped into her chamber, landing cheerfully on her belly. She laughed at its childlike audacity. She peeked under its fluttering wing.

There it was. Another note.

If you desire, the wind will carry you to the beach.

Prissy's heart raced with fear and excitement. Had someone seen her encounter with the wind last night? What awaited her at the beach? Were the wind and the beach related somehow? Who was writing the notes?

She must get to the beach.

She scurried out to the tower, pulling the straps of her nightgown up to their rightful place on her shoulders. Standing in the sunlight in her filmy nightgown suddenly embarrassed her, made her feel too exposed. And yet, she felt energized and free.

If you desire, the wind will carry you to the beach.

Oh, how she desired! The wind was her special friend now. And the beach beckoned with renewed persuasion.

She stood in the daylight with her eyes shut, concentrating on her desire to be at the water's edge. If desiring was her only responsibility, she would do it happily and patiently.

Perhaps it was the heat of the sun, or the intensity of her anticipation, but she lost consciousness. When she was revived, the sounds of the gentle surf greeted her.

She opened her eyes to see a handsome man of her own age kneeling beside her, looking down at her with an expression of kindness and admiration.

"My beautiful Prissy. At last you have come to me!" He said reverently, stroking her cheek.

His eyes were soulful but piercing. Speech eluded her momentarily as she held his gaze, but then she spoke. "Who are you?"

"My name is Orionis, but I would like for you to call me Orio."

"You may call me Pris. How do you know me?"

He chuckled. "I had hoped you might recognize me, but then, too much time has passed for you to remember. We played together as children on this very beach. And then you stopped coming."

"My parents died," she tried to explain.

"Yes. I know. But I longed for you, your beauty, your smile, and your laughter. This day is all I've lived for."

"Why did you wait so long to contact me?" She wished he would touch her face again.

He smiled. "I watched you become a beautiful young woman, day by day, as you sat in your tower. I have certain gifts I wish to give you, Pris, and they require that you be mature enough to receive them. I think you are ready now."

"What kind of gifts?"

"I delivered one last night," he grinned.

"The wind!" She blushed.

He traced his finger up along the valley that separated her thighs and she caught her breath. Even through the fabric of her gown, his touch was like lightning in a thunderstorm. "Did you enjoy it?"

"Oh, yes," she whispered. "Very much."

"I have so much more to give you," he said, moving his face toward hers. Their lips met and she felt the essence of herself meld with his. Although she lay on the ground, some part of her soul soared high above her.

She knew that, as he kissed her, he slipped her nightgown from her body. She did not object for she wanted his hands on her so desperately. How smoothly and swiftly he moved!

His lips were soft yet their power overtook her. She lay like melted ice on the blanket he'd placed on the sand for her. Their tongues found one another, probing and wrapping around each other.

He never stopped kissing her as he undressed her. The warm sun infused her with a delicious liberation.

He took a breast in his hand. After caressing it tenderly for a while, he moved his mouth to her erect, waiting nipple. He licked it gingerly, as if unsure of her pleasure. She stroked his dark hair to convey her approval, prompting him to take her lovely pink nipple into his mouth, where he sucked it hungrily. His busy mouth at her tit ignited her body the way the wind had the night before.

Little sounds came from her throat as he suckled her—sounds she'd never heard herself make in the past. Her body seemed to sizzle from sunshine and desire. His eyes were closed in rapture as his mouth pleasured her. She had never felt such intense fondness for a person, such ethereal delight in anyone's aura.

"Orio," she whispered.

He looked up, concerned. "What's wrong?"

"Nothing. I just wanted to speak your name." She smiled.

He smiled in return and resumed sucking her tit.

He slid his hand slowly down the length of her stomach, tarrying at her navel, following the contours of her womanly curves. His fingers brushed lightly at the blonde tuft of hair between her legs. Her body was so hungry for him. She wanted to spread her legs wide to offer herself but knew she mustn't. Oh, she could not get close enough to this Orio!

He gently separated her legs. She did not fight him. Spreading her legs only as far as his movements prodded her, she gave him access to her needy succulence.

Her sweet, musky scent wafted around them when she opened her legs. It surprised her, but he breathed deeply, as if enjoying the aroma of a gourmet meal. He pressed his nose to her mons area and she jumped a bit. He stroked her thigh to assure her that all was well.

He then got to his feet and stood in the triangle formed by her legs. How strong he looked! He smiled at her with such an endearing mixture of appreciation, sensuality, and lust that she could not help but smile back.

She watched silently as he removed his shirt, exposing his hard, healthy chest to the invigorating sun. Her breathing quickened, for she knew what was to come off next. With marvelous efficiency, he unzipped his pants and stepped out of them. His cock pointed north, like a compass. The servants had told many stories of the penis, and she'd harbored much trepidation about encountering one. But this one drew her to it, made her hungry for it. And she trusted him to be gentle and loving with it.

He knelt between her legs and she saw her hunger reflected in his gaze. He placed his hands on the soft insides of her thighs to open her a bit wider. Then, his face disappeared between her legs. His tongue ran along her labia, which was covered with her juices. He swirled his tongue up to her hard, hot little clit and lapped at it incessantly, going over and over it until she could neither focus nor think. Her wetness spread over his face, and although she could not see what he was doing, she loved the slippery eroticism of it.

When he found her secret slit, he slipped his tongue inside her. She squirmed now, unable to contain the pleasure he gave her.

"Do you like the way I eat you?" he asked from her nether regions.

"Yes, oh yes! Keep eating me, Orio!"

She pushed her juicy center into his face and moved her hips around to increase the sensation of his tongue inside her.

"The taste of you makes me strong, Pris."

His words were too much. She erupted into a powerful orgasm that made her shout and tremble. She grabbed at his hair as if he could keep her earthbound. Her body felt like it had been projected into the heavens and bits of her were scattered among the clouds. He continued to eat her pussy, even as she bucked wildly under his expert mouth. Finally, she could withstand no more and pulled away. She lay gasping and exhausted.

He grinned with his chin shiny from her wet cream.

"I know how to cool you off," he said.

He stood and then picked her up, carrying her like a groom carries a bride. Just before he lifted her, she saw that his cock was bigger and darker than it had been before. She wondered if it was painful for him.

He toted her toward the sea, whose cool waters promised to make her feel human once again. But the waters did little to soothe, for Orio's strong embrace stimulated her. He waded into the Sea of Tranquillity until her bottom was immersed and the water line crossed his chest. They kissed deeply and long as the waves slapped gently at their bodies.

The tip of his cock periodically stabbed at her thigh. She ached to have it penetrate her but was too shy to ask directly.

"I feel something poking at me," she observed shyly.

He raised an eyebrow and gave her a crooked smile. "That would be my cock," he said, clearly aware that his words would turn her on. "It's hard because it needs to be inside you."

"My pussy wants your cock," she whispered, amazed at her brazenness.

With her arms still wrapped around his neck, he skillfully shifted her body so she straddled him in the water. He took hold of her buttocks and lifted her, positioning her sweet hole over the head of his cock. Then he held her hips and pulled her down, impaling her on his tool.

She called out her pleasure. Her pussy was very tight and so his entry was a powerful mix of temporary pain giving way to profound ecstasy. He slid up so far inside her! She clutched his waist with her legs. He pulled her up slightly and brought her down again. As he repeated this, she moved with him, sensing the rhythm. The water intensified their fucking by putting everything in slow motion.

Her wet pussy grabbed at his cock and seemed to suck it into her. Her body was a stream of conscious and unconscious passion, flowing with the current of the sea.

Suddenly, Orio's grip on her hips tightened and the expression of his face became a primal, urgent grimace. When he shouted, his cock twitched inside her, and she realized he was experiencing the same kind of release he'd elicited from her. His pumping cock combined with his orgasmic explosion thrilled her. Her body was once again consumed by undulating waves of pleasure. The couple came together, loudly exclaiming their passion.

When it was over, she nuzzled his neck. Tears of joy threatened to leak from her eyes.

"I have not known happiness like this," she admitted, awed.

He kissed her in reply.

"It is better than I even imagined," he said. "But I am afraid my legs are too weak now for me to continue standing," he chuckled.

She climbed down from him, laughing. They returned to the blanket on the beach and lay face up, worshipping the brilliant sun.

After some moments of quiet recovery, she spoke.

"Do you live on this beach?"

"The beach and the forest. Even on the Precipice of Paradise. I am wherever I need to be."

She had many questions but their answers suddenly held little relevance. This moment and this man were her only concern.

"May I stay here with you?"

"What of Uncle Mikhail?" He teased.

She paused, thinking fondly of her ward. "I have more desire to know what earthly delights may be found in the forest!"

ⅭⅭⅭⅭⅭⓄ

For Want of a Nail

⊰ BY MOLLY LASTER ⊱

T was a crazy thing to have happen, running out of supplies at the last minute like that. Crazy, because generally Viva Diva is a very respectable establishment. We never run out of condoms or lube or fresh three-hundred-thread sheets. There are always extra handcuffs available, as well as extra sets of handcuff keys (the keys are all the same—they fit every pair of cuffs we own—which is something not everyone knows). But on this night, the Saturday of a three-day holiday weekend, the crowds were insane, and when I went running back to the supply room, I was shocked at what I saw.

No More Nails.

That meant that the dominant in room three wasn't going to be able to bind down his nubile young slave using the expensive leather thongs he'd special-ordered from a dirty mail-order French catalog. This particular dom has a unique style. He likes to work with a stripped-bare room. Nothing but a mattress sheathed in rubber and a sturdy wooden chair. He takes it upon himself to hammer hooks into the bed frame, nails into the wood, creating the most spectacular arrangements that are never to be duplicated again. We cater to his wants because he pays our exorbitant prices. Besides, if you've never seen a slave bound down to a chair, watching her Master create the weapons of her impending destruction, then you've missed out on something important in life.

And now, for want of a nail—of a box of heavy-duty standard nails—the evening's take would be much lowered. More seriously than that, for want of a nail, the slave would be lost, crawling submissively off in search of other masters who could take care of her immediate needs and carnal cravings. For want of a slave, the Master would be lost, because Master X rarely allows changes in his planned schedule. For want of his show, the audience would be lost, because all who come to our club like to witness Master X in action, and without him, they would undoubtedly head to other dark arenas. For want of an audience, the reputation would be lost—we never fail our clientele. Not ever. And for want of our reputation, well, the whole gig could be lost.

My head hurt at this thought—all the effort I've put in to create the most perfect sadistically inclined sex club. And for what? The buzz in underground circles would be at an all-time high, and our most beloved customers might jettison us in favor for Noir Rumors, the private club down the street.

"Run," I told Sasha, my redheaded personal assistant who adheres to my every command as if I were her own personal deity. "Run like the wind to the twenty-four-hour hardware store. Get the nails. Run like a motherfucker, my sweet, and be back as soon as you can." I paused, massaging my temples in slow circles. "I'll stall."

"How?" Sasha stammered.

I glared at her, at the impudence in her query, but at the same time, the question echoed in my own head: *How would I?* Master X had demanded the box of nails, he had his hammer, he was ready for action. So I did the only thing I could think of—I offered myself.

This is a rare occurrence, indeed. Yes, I have my own carnal wants just like any other soul who wanders through the glossy red-painted front door of our club. But I take care of mine after hours, which can be quite late indeed. Officially, we close the doors at 2:00 A.M. Unofficially, parties can go on well past dawn. Often, I don't get myself sexually sorted out until daylight fills the windows—or would if they weren't covered with heavy black velvet curtains. *This* was a time for exceptions.

Taking a deep breath, I stalked down the narrow hallway until I reached the largest room. There, the dom was pacing—his boots made clicking sounds on the concrete floor—while his love slave wept silently and the audience watched intently. Was this all part of an act? Or had something gone terribly wrong? I wouldn't give them time to figure that out. I presented myself before the Master, and I said in a voice only he could hear, "Nails are on the way. Until then, I have an offer for you."

His silvery eyes gleamed at me. I didn't verbalize what I was suggesting. Instead, I showed him with my body, stripping slowly out of the black leather dress and letting it fall silently to the floor in an expensive black puddle. My hand was on the bra beneath, but he stopped me.

"Keep those," he said, nodding to the bra, panties, and tall, stiletto-tipped heels. "And only those." Then, gracefully, he bent me over the stripped rubber-sheeted bed and told me to hold myself still.

"No bounds—" someone murmured in the crowd. There was a lot of ambient noise now, as people realized what they were about to witness. I'm rarely part of the show. This would be a memorable night, indeed.

"She doesn't require bondage," another person responded correctly. "She holds herself still."

"But *he's* Master X—"

"And you know who she is. Houdini's opposite. She doesn't like bindings. Lives for the thrill of being unfettered."

This was the truth. I cannot bear to be fastened in place. I hold my own, regardless of the intensity, by keeping a mental monologue in my mind. I obey myself, even as I obey the dominant. That's my deal, my own unspoken arrangement. I'd have it no other way. And, of course, this worked perfectly for the Master, since without nails, how could he have used his special thongs, anyway?

Master X showed me his weapon before letting it meet my skin. He'd chosen a beautiful crop, one of my all-time favorite toys, and he announced to the crowd that they would do him a great service by counting along with the punishment, numbering the blows—and it *was* to be a punishment. I'd failed him, even if the rest of the audience didn't know that, couldn't possibly guess the multilevels of the show we were about to perform.

· I closed my eyes before the first stroke landed, and I found that center inside myself to focus on. I saw the object within my body as a steel-like wire, one burning with a crimson light. An image always helps, like focusing on a flame to calm the soul. Helps, yes—but tonight none of my tricks worked. The pain was as startling and powerful as it always is, yet this time, I couldn't lose myself in the melody of the ache. I was alive and witness to each second of the discipline, almost as if I were outside my body watching. But while calmness usually spreads quickly through me when I'm absorbing a master's pain, tonight I couldn't find my core.

The first blow landed on my raised buttocks, and I shuddered all over as I tried to swallow it down. Tried to contain the power of the blow within myself. The crowd whispered, "One," as if they were a single voice, a solitary unit.

"Two" and "three" fell rapidly, but I didn't twist or turn or try to use my hands to block the pain. I know better. I know my place. Yet I wondered for the first time ever if I would be able to hold my part of the deal. Could I give the Master what he needed?

"Four" and "five" were stinging pokers on my heated flesh. Before the dominant continued, he pulled my leather panties down my thighs, and these he used to keep my legs contained. My ankles were in a twist of leather from the panties, but I could have kicked my way to freedom if I'd wanted. My hands were useless, at my sides, until the Master told me to hold them over my head. He wanted my body elongated, wanted to choose his next place to brand me. Then "six" and "seven," "eight" and "nine," and a blur of blows that had suddenly reached the high teens.

I could feel the tears start to slide free from my eyelids, although I didn't even think that I was crying until the wetness reached my cheeks. Still, I didn't move. I couldn't— I . . . would . . . not.

Where was Sasha? I found myself wondering. For want of a nail . . . one whipping might have been lost. But for lack of a nail, the owner of the club was receiving the whipping of the evening, because now the crop flew faster and the crowd had to hurry to keep up with the numbers.

The cadence of the many voices was what finally gave me the strength I needed. I locked onto the sound, the hypnotic sound of all those voices calling out numbers that were stripes on my skin, and I didn't move. I took my pain as a pro, and only when Sasha finally arrived, falling on her knees before the Master and offering over the box of nails, did I finally realize how well done I was. Stewed in the juices of my pussy that ran down my thighs and coated the bed. I thought that the Master would tell me to remove myself so that he could get to the real work of the night, which is why I found it so surprising when he brought the thongs and the hammer out and bound me down to the bed himself.

Oh, no—I can't.

Can't possibly.

The words blossomed in my head. Can't. No. Not that. Not me. I don't squirm. I don't flinch. But don't tie me. Do not! And then he was on me with the reversal of pain, the thick handle of the crop sliding deep into my pussy. He fucked me with that as powerfully as he'd punished me, using the very weapon he'd whipped me with—and was most likely going to continue to whip me with, as well, once the climax flooded through me. How had this all happened? In the course of an hour, my world had tipped on its side.

The pleasure began to spill out of me, and I turned my head back and forth now, struggling ferociously when I knew I could not possibly get free. Oh, there was delight in that action. Trying to get away, trying to break the bonds, when I knew that struggling would only work somehow to capture them tighter.

After watching me flail, the Master took pity and used

his hands under me, touching my pulsing, swollen clit, spreading my shaved pussy lips so wide apart, so that as I bucked and writhed on the bed, I finally came. Waves of bliss. Unbound, limitless pleasure.

For want of a nail—the club was saved, and a mighty orgasm was had, indeed.

Goldicocks and the Three Pairs

⊣ BY ECHO THOMAS ⊢

NCE upon a time in Berkeley, California, six friends from the university decided to live together after graduation in a three-story townhouse. Jack and Janie lived in the one-bedroom suite on the first floor. They were a fetching wheat-haired couple whose preferences tended toward the polite and middle-class; they ate pasta with bottled tomato sauce and timidly watched soft-core erotica on their bedroom television set. Bill and Bob were a happy pair of redheads with rather more unusual tastes. They sullied the cooperative kitchen with the aroma of spicy curries and spicy Cajun gumbo. They lived on the second floor, where they practiced their particular brand of what might politely be called out-of-the-ordinary exploration.

Kirsten and Katia, both brunettes, occupied the topmost floor of the townhouse; while they certainly appreciated the well-bred quietude of their downstairs neighbors, the more outrageous behavior of Bill and Bob titillated them. Oftentimes Kirsten and Katia would be engaged in an intimate moment only to have their reverie interrupted by the shuddering of the house as Bill and Bob went at it. Though their occasional response would be to pound on the floor, more often they listened intently and took their cues from the adventuresome pair below. Jack and Janie installed sound-absorbent polystyrene sheets on their ceiling, covering them with a giant batik tapestry featuring a colorful couple knotted in an improbable pose from the Kama Sutra, and all three pairs were deliriously happy.

One day, Kirsten and Katia's friend Gigi returned from a yearlong trip to Europe and was invited to stay for a few weeks. The first night of her stay at the townhouse, she was treated to a meal prepared by Jack and Janie (all cooking duties were rotated between the couples in the household). They prepared a porridge of twelve wholly organic grains, topped with brown sugar provided by a Latin American cooperative that paid its farmers a fair market price. To this delicacy was added a thin film of half-and-half produced by free-range cows that received daily rubdowns and aromatherapy. By the time Jack and Janie had explained all this to their dining companions, Gigi noted miserably that the porridge had grown cold.

"Well," said Janie primly. "If we had a microwave you could heat it up, but we all agreed that we don't approve of the use of hazardous radiation to provide household convenience. I hope you don't mind it cold?"

"Not at all," said Gigi politely, spooning some of the congealed brew into her mouth.

"Gigi normally likes it hot. Very hot," teased Katia. Gigi was a curvy blonde who had long politely declined her female friends' invitations to a rendezvous, on the grounds that while she appreciated new experiences, she was not interested in the particular brand of experience the charming lesbian brunettes offered. Despite their mutual respect for their friend's boundaries, Katia and Kirsten couldn't resist teasing Gigi about her rumored proclivities while on her European odyssey; in fact, word had come back to their circle of friends that Gigi had engaged in sordid escapades with men from just about every country in the European continent (and more than a few travelers from lands farther afield). Nonetheless, few if any of these trysts had satisfied her, and she'd earned a nickname for her fondness for discarding lovers as quickly as she tempted them into her embrace. Her friends called her "Goldicocks."

"I'm looking for one that's just right," giggled Gigi as she flirted over the sodden remains of the twelve-grain porridge.

"Baby, I've got your 'just right' upstairs," winked Katia. "Third floor, hang a left at the Tracy Chapman poster. Seven different sizes, all made of medical-grade silicone."

"Honey," laughed Bill, "You don't know the meaning of the word 'just right.' Size does matter, don't you know?"

This caused Jack and Janie to blush a fierce red, but not before Gigi's eyes had locked on Jack's and she had spied the meaningful glance that passed between Jack and Janie. When the six housemates trundled off to bed, Gigi burrowed under her organic-cotton sleeping bag on the living-room futon with her tie-dyed T-shirt rubbing suggestively against her nipples. Gigi couldn't deny that her long trip (and the unsatisfying meal of free-range fair-market-price organic porridge) had left her more than a little hungry for stimulation.

She waited for the house to quiet, then slipped on her Tevas and tiptoed down the hall to Jack and Janie's room. The thoughtful couple had left the door open for her.

Gigi found Jack and Janie propped up in bed watching a suggestive video that consisted entirely of women in expensive lingerie eating fruit while men in pirate outfits watched.

"Come to bed, sweetie," cooed Janie, more brashly than she was used to. "Want some more porridge?"

"Um, thanks . . . I'm stuffed. Couldn't eat another bite."

Janie's kiss was tender, warm, and Jack's hands roved over Gigi's body, slipping up the long tie-dyed T-shirt and caressing her well-furred pussy. Gigi moaned softly as the friendly couple stripped her of everything but her Tevas, not wanting to interfere with her sense of independence. Janie's lips still smacked of brown sugar, and she teased her sticky-sweet tongue into Gigi's receptive mouth while Jack suckled on the guest's firm breasts. The two of them watched lingerie-clad women eat fruit and had a mutually respectful session of erotic cuddling and spirited but non-exploitative fondling. While Gigi certainly found herself open to the new experience this presented, she did notice herself at times making a mental catalog of the cracks in the ceiling, seized unexpectedly with a curious desire to return with some spackle.

When she kissed Jack and Janie good-bye just before dawn, she found herself puzzling over the dissatisfied pulsing in her loins as she tossed and turned on the living-room futon.

"That pair was *too soft*," she grumbled when she awoke well after noon.

After a long day of job- and house-hunting, Gigi returned to the townhouse and enjoyed a group meal. Bill and Bob had cooked up their extra-special seventeen-alarm vegetarian black-bean chili for the household, and while their four housemates yelped and moaned in agony, Gigi found herself devouring bowl after bowl, profoundly satisfied by the relentless attack of the organic habaneros that festooned the spicy concoction.

She caught both Bill and Bob letting their eyes linger over the skintight Prague Film Festival crop-top she wore, her nipples showing braless and erect from the unstoppable onslaught of the chili. Maybe they were just curious?

Nonetheless, as she'd read in human sexuality class, spicy food aroused carnal impulses in humans, and she certainly found that to be true. Shortly after the housemates went to sleep, Gigi dug through the box she'd retrieved from her storage locker and put on a pair of stilettos and a red nightie with Betty Boop embroidered above the left breast. She tiptoed upstairs and found Bill and Bob's bedroom door open.

The place was furnished in black leather, with a sling and a fifty-five-gallon drum of vegetable shortening set up near the window. Shimmering metal eyebolts adorned every beam and baseboard. Bill and Bob were stretched nude on the leather-covered bed, Bill with his boots still on.

"Look, darling," he said. "We have a new playmate. What's your name, dollface?"

"Just call me Goldicocks," giggled Gigi, thinking surely that men such as Bill and Bob could appreciate the nickname.

They could, without a doubt. They seized Gigi passionately and guided her to her knees, Bob handcuffing her as Bill teased the tip of his big boot into her mouth.

"Lick my boots, slave," he growled.

Gigi had never licked boots before, though she'd certainly done plenty of the other things the couple invited her to do. Leather tasted particularly unusual, but Bob's cock, in particular, tasted quite nice. Bill's, however, was rather bigger than she'd expected, and when the two lovers lifted Gigi into the sling and manacled her there spread-eagled and suspended with her behind lifted in a quite improbable posture, she found herself yelping at the unexpected magnitude of Bill's penetration of her entrance, which had previously restricted its invitations, primarily, to southern European and Mediterranean visitors.

"Too fast, honey?"

"Um," she said. "Too . . . *something.*"

Bill moderated his bunnylike pounding for a moment, but found it difficult to stop calling their sling-bound guest a "little slut" and a "cock-hungry fag hag." The affectionate epithets didn't bother her on principle, but she did suffer a moment of abject terror when Bob's fervent pistoning of his man-sized plumbing caused the eyebolts in the ceiling to rip free, sending the trio tumbling into a situation what Bill insisted on referring to—his political incorrectness apparently a matter of little, if any, concern—as a "Mongolian clusterfuck."

When Gigi tiptoed downstairs at dawn she found herself minus one stiletto and with a favorite red nightie that had been reduced to a tangled snake's nest of shreds. She'd certainly reached her completion numerous times on the impressive enormity of Bill's maleness, and Bob had certainly provided her with all the fellatial gratification she would be needing anytime soon. But she found her bones creaking uncomfortably as she slipped nude and lube-smeared under her all-cotton blanket, and when she awakened in the morning to lather herself up with Dr. Bronner's soap, she discovered that vegetable oil was not nearly as biodegradable as Bill and Bob had been led to believe. And it was a *bitch* to get come out of one's eyebrows.

"That pair was *too hard*," pronounced Gigi.

All day she shopped for organic produce from the grocery list Kirsten had provided, and she noticed repeatedly how the multiply-pierced and simply adorable checkers at the natural foods store kept making eyes at her from beneath their filmy curtains of primary-colored bangs.

That night Kirsten and Katia cooked vegetarian coq au vin, and Gigi had never tasted anything so delicious. She actually found herself moaning faintly with each bite, so intoxicating was this new and different use of soybean products.

"Come upstairs tonight," whispered Katia. "We'll make you moan some more."

Perhaps naively, Gigi squirmed into her Girl Power T-shirt before tiptoeing up to the third floor. The door to Bill and Bob's room was shuddering magnificently, and from beyond it she could hear the tortured strains of "Yes, Daddy, please, Daddy, more, Daddy," which made her tiptoe upstairs appreciably faster.

Katia and Kirsten were waiting for her in stilettos and fishnets—Katia in white, Kirsten in black.

"Oh, look, darling," cooed Kirsten. "Girl Power."

"I think she's so sweet," sighed Katia. "We should do something nice for her."

"Tsk, tsk," said Kirsten. "I think she's naughty. We should do something really *mean*."

"How about a little of each?" said Gigi.

Kirsten and Katia sandwiched Gigi enthusiastically between them, their hands roving everywhere as they stripped off her Girl Power T-shirt and whispered, "I'll show you Girl Power, *Goldicocks*." Gigi found herself first over Kirsten's knee, then Katia's, their firm but skilled hands providing a wealth of new experiences. When they bound her to the bed with her ass high in the air, Katia managed to select just the right size of cock to slip into her patent-leather harness. Gigi sighed with pleasure as Katia entered her, her mouth working eagerly between Kirsten's spread legs. The bed creaked in angry protest as they drove its structural integrity to the edge, but remained sound no matter how many times it groaned.

When Gigi awakened at dawn, she found herself snuggled between the two naked lesbians, locked in an embrace that would have taken quite a bit of effort to break. She knew that for the sake of propriety she ought—in theory— to tiptoe down to the living room and toss and turn on the futon for a while in utter dissatisfaction—out of politeness to her previous playmates.

Then she figured: What the fuck? She squirmed deeper into the embrace of her sleeping friends, drawing a deep breath of their luxurious scent. There really wasn't any reason to go downstairs, she mused. After all, she'd found exactly what she was looking for: she'd have to change her nickname.

"This pair was *just right*," sighed Goldicocks, and went back to sleep.

ⓒⓒⓒⓒⓒ

Hannah & Greta

⇥ BY ERIN SANDERS ⇤

NCE upon a time in Los Angeles there lived a pair of exotic dancers from Finland named Hannah and Greta. They had been best friends since their childhood in a small Lapland town well north of the Arctic Circle, and they worked together at a club on Hollywood Boulevard called Hollywood North. Despite its name, there was very little Nordic about the club. Most of the dancers were salon-tanned, bottle-blonde and silicone-enhanced. Hannah and Greta, however, had retained the milk-white skin and jet-black hair that spoke of their homeland at the top of the world, and their slender bodies remained free from surgical enhancements. However, each sported a tattoo: Hannah's name on Greta's pretty behind, and Greta's name on Hannah's.

The kind customers at Hollywood North adored Hannah and Greta, turning out to see their shows every night, cheering enthusiastically at the very sight of the girls' lustrous coal-black hair or the slim curve of their nude bodies. Whenever Hannah and Greta would appear, the customers rained ten- and twenty-dollar bills down onstage or tucked them shyly into the matching black latex G-strings the two girls wore. When Hannah would lean in close and kiss Greta (sort of), their tongues snaking out and undulating suggestively with only the barest hint of a touch, the chipped linoleum stage would become a tossed salad of tens, twenties, and hundreds. Hannah and Greta were very happy, and the customers were even happier.

What's more, despite their obvious success, Hannah and Greta were so kind, gentle, and considerate that they were favorites of the other dancers, who tended, normally, to be rather catty toward each other (especially the most successful girls). Hannah and Greta never failed to clean up after themselves in the dressing room, and almost never complained or said a bad word about anyone. They even liked the customers, giggling to each other each night about what a good time they'd had lap-dancing before they went out for a cup of coffee at Madge's Diner and then went home to their one-bedroom cottage in West Hollywood, nestled between the gay couple with three dogs and the screenwriter finishing his masterpiece.

The owner of the club, however, was married to a bitter washed-up porn star whose body had been tanned in a salon until it had wrinkled up and browned to an unnatural hue. She was constantly complaining about Hannah and Greta, and saying that if they would only visit a tanning salon their pale skin wouldn't hurt her ancient eyes whenever they took the stage. What's worse, the customers who so adored Hannah and Greta were so excited about throwing their money onto the stage or tucking it into Hannah's and Greta's G-strings that they forgot all about buying drinks, and as a result the club was now under some financial strain.

The owner was a kindly man, but he was meek in response to his wife's constant nagging. He finally agreed to take action, and went to Hannah and Greta as they were counting their money after a particularly successful evening.

"We, um, have an in-store performance at a smut shop in the Valley," he said guiltily. "A limo will come by your apartment to pick you up at noon."

Hannah and Greta giggled and jumped up and down with enthusiasm—they had never had an in-store performance. "What should we wear?" they perkily asked the owner.

"Um . . . bikinis," he said with a look of shame on his face. "And bring tanning oil."

"Tanning oil?" puzzled Hannah and Greta, but the owner had already slithered off miserably to tell his wife the news.

When the limousine picked up Hannah and Greta at noon, they were still rubbing the sleep out of their eyes as they climbed into the limousine wearing only their matching white bikinis. The driver took them deep into the Valley, taking the 110 to the 5 to the 505 and then merging onto the 810 before shuffling north on the 15. Hannah and Greta had begun to suspect something was not as it seemed. When the limousine pulled off the freeway, the two girls whispered to each other.

"You'd better watch the street signs," said Hannah, who was somewhat nearsighted and never wore her glasses when performing.

"In case we need to get back," said Greta, nodding.

The limousine driver took them through a tangled maze of streets, which Hannah cataloged in her brain. But when the driver pulled up into a strip mall and stopped at the shop marked TANNING SALON, they received an unexpected disappointment.

"Quick," Hannah said. "Do you know how we get back?"

"Surely," said Greta. We take a left on Kiywokma and then a right on Iompazol, and then we bear left on Zuzu Moroni! Then it's just a straight shot on the 51 north to the 18, then it's all about the 11 until we get back to West Hollywood!"

"Oh, shit," said Hannah, who had forgotten that her best friend was dyslexic.

"We'll never get home!" said Greta, feeling guilty.

"Don't worry!" said Hannah, and comforted Greta with a tender French kiss.

The two girls nervously entered the tanning salon.

"Hello?" asked Greta. "We're here for the in-store appearance!" Finding no one in the shop, they went together down the hallway that led to the tanning booths.

Suddenly the owner's wife appeared and barred the door behind them. "Hah! Now I've got you!" She shoved Hannah into one of the booths and slammed the door while Greta gaped, astonished.

Snapping handcuffs on Greta's wrists, the owner's wife cackled as she turned the tanning booth on HIGH. "I'm going to cook that fish-belly slut into the prettiest little beach bunny you ever did see," she said. "And then she's going to dance for me!" The owner's wife leaned close to Greta and said, "And you're next, penguin girl!"

Greta was so upset by the thought of her best friend cooked all brown by the owner's wife that she neglected to point out that there were damned few penguins in Finland. Tears formed in Greta's eyes as the owner's wife forced her into the back storeroom and locked the door. But the clever Greta noticed that the circuit breaker was tucked into a corner of the storeroom, and she climbed on top of a giant can of tanning oil and with her perky nose flipped the breaker that said TANNING BOOTH.

The owner's wife checked on Hannah after an hour, but when Hannah obediently put her behind up against the glass panel of the tanning booth, it was discovered by the owner's wife to be as pearly white as when she began.

"Damn," grumbled the owner's wife. "She has less melanin than I thought. This is going to take a while."

Hannah had figured out that the tanning booth was not working properly and was trying to figure out a way to escape. Meanwhile, Greta had found a transom window in the back storeroom and, still handcuffed, wriggled out through it, tearing off her bikini in the process. Now nude, she went around to the front of the shop.

"Help! Help!" she said as a handsome computer millionaire in an Aston-Martin SUV pulled into the tanning salon.

"Good lord!" said the millionaire, amazed to discover a brunette stripper waiting for him handcuffed and nude as he entered the tanning salon. "I don't remember calling ahead for entertainment!"

Tears in her eyes, Greta begged the millionaire for help. "My boss's evil wife has trapped my best friend in the booth! She's trying to give her a tan!"

"How awful!" said the millionaire. "I assume she doesn't want one?"

"No, no," wept Greta. "She looks just like me. We're *happy* being pale!"

"And I'm happy with you pale, too," said the millionaire, giving Greta's naked body a lustful and devouring glance.

Bewitched by the millionaire's handsomeness, Greta fell into his embrace, producing in him an immediate erection and a fervent desire to help this handcuffed exotic dancer no matter what the cost.

"I'll save your friend," said the millionaire, and tiptoed deep into the shop.

Hannah had managed to tear away a section of the tanning booth's Naugahyde lining. She stretched it over her rear end, and when the owner's wife came up cackling, "Let's see, my pretty! Let's see if you're cooked brown yet!" Hannah put her butt up against the tanning booth window with the cracked brown covering stretched over it.

"Perfect!" shrieked the owner's wife, whipping open the tanning booth.

Hannah, who had taken self-defense courses, planted an uppercut right on the wife's face. At that moment, the millionaire rushed into the room and kicked the wife squarely in the butt as Hannah jumped out of the tanning booth.

"No!" shrieked the owner's wife. "I'm as tan as I need to be!"

"Gee," said Hannah. "I think someone I know has said *that* before, bitch!"

Greta ran into the back and flipped the circuit breaker. The tanning booth hummed to life, and the owner's wife shrieked and disappeared into a puff of smoke.

"Thank you, thank you!" said Hannah and Greta as

they showered the millionaire with kisses. "What ever can we do to repay you?"

"I can think of a few things," said the handsome millionaire lasciviously.

When they returned many hours later to the club the owner wept with relief, embracing them and saying, "I thought she'd tan you for sure!"

"We made her disappear in a puff of smoke!" said Greta.

"Yeah, we really cooked her goose!"

"Oh, thank God!" said the owner, glad to be rid of his wife. "I'm sorry I ever listened to her! Please, please say you'll continue to dance at my club!" begged the owner.

"Just the way we are?" asked Hannah suspiciously.

"Yes, yes!" said the owner. "Just the way you are!"

And so Hannah and Greta returned to Hollywood North, dancing with their milk-white skin intact. They married the millionaire, living in a ménage à trois in his mansion at the top of Mulholland. The millionaire was so enamored of his new wives that he visited them every night, watching them dance, and cheering loudest of all when their tongues just barely touched. He even brought his millionaire friends to show off his beautiful new wives, and they all drank like fishes, so even the strip club owner was happy.

And they all lived erotically ever after!

If the Stiletto Fits

⇥ BY K.C. ⇤

o like check it out. Cindy Pascarella is this total goth chick who like freaks us all out, totally. We all knew she didn't have a date for
the homecoming dance, because she is like totally O.T.T. in the *WEIRD* department. Like she's not bad-
looking, I mean, if you're into tall and slim and pale and
stuff, but she never talks to *any* fucking one, she just sits
there at lunch reading weird books by sickos like Sylvia
Plath and that dead guy from Nick Cave and the Bad Seeds,
and writing in this little book of poetry she has. (Carrie
Russo told me she once got Cindy to let her read some of
her poetry and it was like *so weird!!*) She's totally poor because her mother died and she lives with her grandparents
and stuff. She was held back a year after doing an exchange
program, so she's already nineteen, a year older than me.
Actually, she's older than everyone, except Brett Naylor
who flunked third grade, like, twice. A year ago she tried to
get all her teachers to call her Cynthia instead of Cindy but
none of us care because we've been in school with her
since first grade, okay, so to me, like, forget it, once you've

been Cindy that long you're going to be Cindy for life, just
give it up, *goth girl!!!* Cindy Cindy Cindy!!

So the *LAST* thing any of us expected was to see her at
the homecoming dance screwing Kayla Carter's *BOY-
FRIEND!!*

Okay, so nobody saw it except me, so you can just get all
self-righteous and say I'm lying because Brett Naylor is
such a good guy and he'd never fool around on Kayla, especially not with a *FREAK* like Cindy, but whatever. I don't
blame him, Kayla is a total bitch and always has been, like
that time in seventh grade she told everyone I was a lezzie
just because I liked Melissa Etheridge. I mean CHRIST, I
don't even like her anymore!! Anyway, K. was still such a
bitch to me and totally talked shit to her friends about me,
but fuck her.

Anyway, so it's, like, an hour into the dance and of
course everyone is totally trashola, I mean, I've had like six
wine coolers and I'm feeling all warm and happy and we're
dancing to, like, Britney and Avril and stuff, but I have to
say that Jake Armbruster is like a total *LOSER*. I thought
he was totally cute is why I asked him to the dance, but all
he did was get totally trashed and lose it everywhere in the
limousine. But that came later.

Okay, so Krissi and Jordyn and Katrinka and I are all
like dancing out there while Jake and all his loser friends
do beer bongs with J.D. in the bathroom, and Kayla and
Brett are like slow-dancing to fast songs, PUH-LEEZE, all
showing off 'cause Kayla just KNOWS she's gonna be voted
Homecoming Queen of the Fucking Universe, probably
'cause she blew every guy who voted, SLUT!! I swear to
God I never wanted to see as much of Kayla's tongue as I

did that night, and I have to say that Brett looked like he was kind of over it.

Anyway, so we all go outside to sneak a smoke and you are *not* going to believe what happens. Real slow, like, this total stretch white limousine pulls up, okay I am not talking like one of those normal jobs like what Jake and his friends rented, we are talking *vintage*. Like, it had a historical plate on it which Jake keeps telling me is sooooooo cool 'cause it means it's all old. And I saw this Rolls-Royce logo on the hood of it.

So this driver gets out of the front and you are not going to believe what she was wearing. Yeah, I'm not kidding, it was a girl driver. She had on like this skintight catsuit and these big combat boots and one of those little chauffeur's caps but in LEATHER. I am not fucking kidding. And she looks like a fashion model or something, except for all the piercings. But the driver wasn't half of what was weird about it, because she gets out of the driver's side and opens the door of the limo, and Guess. Who. Steps. Out.

Cindy. Fucking. Pascafuckingrella. Slut of the universe.

Okay, so, like, picture Marilyn Manson's girlfriend crossed with one of those postcards of Hillary Clinton in, like, a tight black thing carrying a whip and shit. Okay, so Cindy didn't have a whip, but she might as well have. She had on this really tight thing that totally had her tits spilling out with all these laces back and forth across them and it TOTALLY showed her belly. Of course she's totally got this pierced belly button. And her legs are, like, practically bare, she's got on this SLUT skirt that shows everything including these black garters that go down to black fishnets that don't even START until three inches underneath the hem of the skirt. But that's cool cause you can see EVERY INCH of those slutty fishnets because Cindy is wearing—You. Have. To. Believe. Me.—knee-high SEE-THROUGH!!!! boots, like they're made out of glass or some high-tech plastic or something, with all these buckles going down the side. Oh. My. God. And they've got six-inch heels so she's like towering over everyone because none of us would ever wear fuck-me-heels like that to HOMECOMING!!!

Anyway, she's got this black fur wrap around her shoulders and her black hair's all teased out and slutty and she is GLITTERING with diamonds—I mean, they had to be real the way they flashed in the light. All over her neck, hanging from her ears, on her fingers, and in her navel. She's a fucking diamond factory. And she's got LOTS of makeup on—heavy blue eyeliner and this TOTALLY dark red lipstick that makes her look real freaky like something out of *Interview with a Vampire*. And this chauffeur of hers who looks like something out of *The Crow* like totally grabs her and gets all close.

"Eleven forty-five" is all she says.

And then she fucking KISSES!!! Cindy Pascarella right on the lips, with TONGUE and everything!!! Then she slaps her on the BUTT!! I mean, we are talking total lezzage here. Okay, by now we're all, like, totally freaked out, and Missy Taylor like starts giggling and says, "Nice outfit, *CIN-DY!!*"

"Eat me," says Cindy Pascarella, and she grabs her crotch.

"Lezzie," Missy says.

"Bulimic," Cindy says, and strides right past us and into the dance—WITHOUT A DATE!

So we went totally wild—this was the weirdest thing

that had ever happened at any dance we'd ever heard of. Missy and Krissi and stuff were, like, all mad and stuff, calling her a freak and stuff, which she is, but I didn't tell them that I thought her outfit was kind of cool. Not that I would ever wear anything like it, not to a SCHOOL DANCE anyway, but I didn't say any of that, I just giggled along with them, and then Missy pulled out this little silver flask of Stoli she had sneaked in and we all got even MORE trashed. When I get trashed, I'm like, a total chain-smoker so we stayed out there for a long time because I knew Jake was praying to the porcelain god and I was NOT going to go hold his long hair the way Krissi did for me that one time I yakked at band camp freshman year.

By the time we went back in, there was this weird thing happening. Kayla is walking around all pissed off looking like she is going to KILL someone. That bitch has not said two words to me since eighth grade, but she grabs the front of my dress and says, "Have you seen Brett?"

I should have said something totally mean, but all I thought of to say was, "No. Why should I know where your fucking boyfriend is?"

"You see him, you tell him it's almost time for the announcement, he'd BETTER be here!"

And Kayla just shoves me, I mean SHOVES me, and if Krissi hadn't caught me I would have, like, totally fallen everywhere. Kayla walks off all fuming and Krissi's like, "What's with her?" And Krissi walks off after Kayla, shouting, "Hey, Kayla, check in the men's room, you'll fit right in there!"

Okay, so I was kind of freaked out and I did NOT want to be around if Kayla and Brett went ballistic, but Krissi was already gone and the others had walked on so I just kind of ducked through this door feeling all weird and teary, I mean Kayla hasn't talked to me in four years and now she's shoving me and shit.

I end up in this stock room or something, all stacked to the ceiling with cans of pineapple and boxes that say FOOD-STUFFS. And you are NOT going to believe what I saw.

Cindy. Fucking. Pascarella. And Brett. Fucking. Naylor.

Cindy's sitting on one of those big FOODSTUFFS boxes, and Brett is all over her, kissing her on the lips while she's got her hand on his tie, holding him. She's rubbing his crotch and Mister Woody has shown up big-time. I'm just standing there watching and they can't really see me that good because I'm behind some of those boxes, and Cindy Pascarella grabs Brett and shoves him down, like SHOVES him onto his knees, and leans back on the boxes with this big smile on her face.

"Lick my boots, bitch," she says.

I am NOT kidding. It's totally like something of late-night HBO. And Brett DOES it. He bends down and takes Cindy Pascarella's knee-high plastic stiletto boots in his hands and starts licking them, all over, just licking, and he's moaning and Cindy's laughing a little, and before I know it she's unbuckling one of her boots and Brett's taking them off and he is TOTALLY licking her BARE FOOT!! Cindy totally spreads her legs and hikes up her skirt and she is NOT wearing ANY PANTIES!!! Like, nothing at all, and she is totally pierced down there. I do NOT need to tell you what happened next. Brett totally starts to go down on her.

Okay, so I'd seen porno and stuff but I'd never watched it for real up close. I guess I was kind of drunk, because it started to feel kind of good. I leaned against the boxes and . . . okay, so this is the part you TOTALLY have to swear NEVER to tell ANYONE!!! I mean, like, stick a needle in your eye, cross your heart and you better hope to die because I will fucking KILL you if you say one word!!!

I got my hand under my dress and started touching it. Down there.

Okay, I knew all about orgasms but I'd never had one, and they covered masturbation in that stupid class they made us take sophomore year, but of COURSE I had never actually DONE it. I don't know what came over me, it just kind of happened. I was all wet and sloppy down there. It started feeling really good.

Cindy was moaning, and Brett starts opening his pants and hauling out Mister Happy, totally stroking it while he really goes to town on Cindy Pascarella. Then Cindy snaps her fingers and says, "Don't touch your cock. Don't fucking touch your cock, Brett."

And Brett just takes his hand off his thing, just letting it hang there while he slides his hands under Cindy's ass and just does it, I mean, like he was LOVING every MINUTE of it. Cindy's all moaning and that's when I realize I'm moaning a little too. And Cindy hears me. She looks over toward me where my head is popping up over the boxes and she just locks eyes with me, and I swear I should have run like hell but for some reason I didn't, I just stood there looking into her eyes while she panted and moaned and then you are NOT going to believe what happened, or at least what I think happened, but Cindy Pascarella grabbed Brett's hair and like rammed her hips up against his face and ground her pussy into his mouth and then she totally

CAME. I mean, we're talking orgasm central. It looked like she was fucking his face, and Brett rode her till the very last instant, or at least I think he did because after the first few seconds my vision went all blurry and I rubbed myself harder and then . . . I think I did it, too.

Oh. My. God. You have GOT to have an orgasm. It feels sooooooo good, and Cindy Pascarella was staring right at me when I did it. Then Brett looked up from Cindy's pussy and his face was totally covered in her lipstick and like all shiny with her pussy juice. He looked right at me, too, and this look of guilt came over his face. I totally freaked out and pulled down my dress and turned and ran.

Outside, they were just starting to announce the Homecoming Queen and King. My legs were all unsteady so I found a chair and plopped into it and looked around to make sure no one saw me come out of the storeroom. They start announcing it, Mr. Beemer being all bald and weird as he reads the names and then you already know what happened—they totally announced Brett and Kayla as the happy couple.

Brett must have heard his name because he comes stumbling out of the storeroom still holding Cindy Pascarella's boot and his clothes are totally messed up and his face is like totally WET. Not to mention being covered in Cindy's red lipstick. He stumbles up onto the stage and everyone's laughing and Kayla doesn't even notice at first and she kisses him and then—OMG, you should have seen the look on her face.

Okay, I missed what happened next, but I hear it was pretty fucking good. Kayla Carter tasting Cindy Pascarella's pussy on her boyfriend's face. But I missed it because just then Cindy darted past me, limping all weird on one stiletto heel and one bare foot, and she locks eyes with me just as she passes me, then runs out the door.

I don't know why I did it, but I ran after her.

I got there just as she's standing there over this smashed pumpkin shouting, "Shit! Shit! Shit!" And it looks like she's totally in shadow or something, because her dress is totally weird-looking, like it's starting to fall apart. She starts running, limping on her one stiletto heel, and disappears around the side of the building.

So I walk over to the pumpkin and look at it, and it's got this deranged face carved on it—I mean, what's up? Halloween was, like, *weeks* ago.

I ran after Cindy but she was already gone. I was sooooo totally trashed. I just sat down on the side of the building and totally freaked out. But then Brett comes running out, his clothes all messed up, and he's holding this ratty old combat boot and screaming, "Cindy! Cindy!" Then he sits down on the side of the building next to me and stuffs his face in the boot, totally *SNIFFING* like it was perfume. I am NOT making this up!!

He totally passes out and I just tiptoe back into the dance pretending I didn't see him.

Okay, so the end of the story is that weirdo Cindy Pascarella came over and sat next to me today in civics class. Like, totally out of her assigned seating, not even caring that Mrs. Harris was going to kick her ass, but then Mrs. Harris never says shit to Cindy because I think she's totally freaked out by her.

So Cindy's writing in her book of poetry like she's not paying attention, but I am totally freaking out. Then she says, just sweet as pie: "Did you have a good time at the dance?"

I shrugged. "It was okay." It seemed really weird not to ask anything back. So after a while I say, "How about you?"

"Oh," says Cindy. "I had a *blast*."

I tried not to laugh, but I couldn't help it. "Yeah, it looked that way. I think they found Brett's body upstate."

And Cindy just giggles, something I don't think I heard the weirdo do since junior high. I turn and look at her and you know, I never really noticed before but she *is* kind of pretty, you know? If you're into freaks.

And she just makes this face at me, like she purses her lips and smiles at me, just totally smiles still wearing that dark red lipstick she smeared all over Brett Naylor's face before she made him eat her pussy. I wonder what that felt like?

"Want to read my poetry?" she asks me.

⊂⊂⊂⊂⊃

Jo White and Cocksucker Red

✥ BY XAVIER ACTON ✥

OSEPHINE White lived in off-campus housing with a Spanish graduate student named Madre. One day at the beginning of the new semester, one of Madre's friends from Barcelona came to stay with Madre for a few weeks. His name was Ursus, and Jo was enchanted by his lustrous black hair and full lips. Jo and Ursus, had a torrid fling on Jo's futon, but soon Ursus had to return to Spain. The next week Jo received a small package by airmail; it was a tube of lipstick in the brightest shade of red Jo had ever seen, with a note from Ursus commenting that perhaps this would make Jo White's lips even *more* kissable, as if that were possible! Flattered, Jo donned the bright red lipstick, shouldered her backpack, and went off to class.

As she was passing behind the natural sciences building, she saw a bearded man dressed in a turtleneck sweater and tweed jacket sitting on a bench. "That's very nice lipstick, sweetie," said the bearded man. "Do you know what we call that where I come from?"

Jo White shook her head.

"We call it cocksucker red," said the bearded man, and unzipped his pants.

Eager to try out her new lipstick and feeling more than a little horny with all the thoughts of her Spanish lover that had filled her mind of late, Jo (who had never been blessed with a talent for fidelity in any event) eagerly dropped to her knees behind the natural sciences building and took the bearded man's cock into her mouth. He moaned softly as she left trails of cocksucker-red lipstick up and down his pole. Soon Jo had satisfied the bearded man, at least physically.

"Hah!" scowled the bearded man. "You call that a blowjob? You'd better get a new shade of lipstick, sweetie!"

This hurt Jo White's feelings, as she'd always considered herself quite accomplished at the arts of oral love, and had received no complaints from any of her previous lovers—least of all Ursus, who had complimented her on her skilled use of the "butterfly." Tears in her eyes, Jo went to class and stewed angrily, wondering if perhaps the bearded man was right and she wasn't quite as good as she thought she was.

The next day, as Jo was heading toward her econ class, she passed behind the psychology building and encountered the bearded man again.

"I see you're wearing your lipstick again," said the bearded man, unbuckling his belt. "Look, girl, I'll give you another chance." He dropped his pants and Jo, who was hoping to receive a passing grade in cocksucking from the bearded man (or at least have him acknowledge her skills as adequate) descended to her knees and took the bearded man's balls into her red-painted mouth, tonguing them gently while he stroked his big cock until he came all over her.

"You call that teabagging?" scoffed the bearded man, zipping up his pants. "I hope your boyfriend isn't very discriminating."

Tears once again formed in Jo's eyes, and she fumed and fumed as she sat through her boring econ class. She resolved to compose an e-mail to Ursus asking him to be honest and tell her whether she gave decent blowjobs. She was crushed the next morning when she didn't find a response to her e-mail; perhaps this was because Ursus didn't want to hurt her feelings.

The next day, Jo was passing behind the performing arts building as she walked to her drama class. She once again encountered the bearded man, who laughed and pulled out his cock when he saw her.

"You again, and still wearing that lipstick! I'll tell you what, let's see if you can deep-throat worth a damn. Deal?"

Jo had always considered deep-throating one of her greatest skills as a lover, not to mention one of her favorite activities. She dropped to her knees and cheerfully took the bearded man's cock down her throat. But no sooner had the bearded man climaxed in Jo's mouth than he snorted in disgust. "You call that deep-throating? I've had better head from my wife!"

Jesus Christ, thought Jo White. *This guy found someone stupid enough to marry him?*

Jo saw a man coming down the path from the performing arts building and went to get off her knees. Before she could, however, she realized that the man was Ursus, and her face reddened as he caught her with the bearded man's pants down.

Ursus gaped in shock. "Jo! Where have you been? I've been looking all over for you!"

"I had to go to class," said Jo White, still kneeling before the bearded man, who looked as shocked as anyone. She struggled to her feet but the bearded man tried to push her back down, whispering lasciviously, "I'll give you one more chance if you do it while your boyfriend watches!"

"Your e-mail turned me on so much I hopped the first plane I could get from Barcelona!" said Ursus. "I *had* to make love to you again."

"Um, Ursus," said Jo. "Listen, I can explain what I'm doing sucking somebody else off," she said. "Um . . . really I can."

"Don't worry about it," said Ursus. "We Barcelonans aren't possessive. But why the hell are you blowing *this* asshole?"

"You know him?"

"He's my admissions counselor!" said Ursus. "Talk about a guy with his panties up his ass-crack! He's the one who refuses to let me transfer my units from Spain! That's why I can't go to school here!"

"What an asshole!" said Jo. "And the son of a bitch wouldn't know a good blowjob if it bit him on the schlong!"

The bearded man cleared his throat and said, "I can explain everything."

"I bet you can," said Ursus. "But that's okay, I'll explain it to your wife, first."

"Really," said the bearded man. "I'm sure we can work something out."

Ursus's eyes narrowed. "I'm sure we can."

With that, he pushed the bearded man onto his knees and guided Jo White onto a park bench where she spread her legs as Ursus forced the admissions counselor's face into Jo's pussy. After a few minutes of tonguing, Jo White stifled a yawn and said, "I guess I don't need to take this guy's opinions on oral sex too seriously, Ursus."

"I guess not," said Ursus, who had proven during his time on Jo White's futon that *his* skills in the language of cunnilingus were not in question. "And I think he's having second thoughts about those Spanish credits, too. Here comes his wife!"

With that, Jo skipped class and she and Ursus went home to tryst on her futon, with Jo's cocksucker-red lipstick going to good use and Ursus practicing his English lessons between Jo White's thighs. The admissions counselor grudgingly accepted Ursus's Spanish credits, allowing him to transfer to the university, where he moved in with Jo, and the two of them lived happily ever after well into graduate school.

King's Counting House

BY JULIA MOORE

 thought it was a place where he did business. That's how naive I was. The building behind Marcus King's refurbished Victorian looked like a cross between a greenhouse and a potting shed, but Marcus always called it "The Counting House." Did he count his money there? Or run numbers for his extremely successful Internet business? I didn't know, and to be perfectly honest, I didn't really care. I don't have the patience to talk about work in my downtime. Not after putting in upward of seventy hours a week, myself. Leave the work alone, I say. Pay attention to me. That's my mantra in any romantic relationship.

But I must admit that at some point I began to get curious. Not Bluebeard's-wife curious, but my interest as to what went on out there was definitely piqued. So I asked.

"Private," Marcus said.

"Private?" I repeated, my long legs spread over his lap, my head leaning back on the gold-brocade sofa. (One of Marcus's best features is how adept he is at decorating.) "Precisely *how* private? Lock and key forever? Or until you know me a little bit better . . . ?" I twirled a strand of my dark, curly hair around one finger as I spoke. I hoped that I looked casual in my questioning, hoped that I didn't betray precisely how interested I was in what he had to say. I've learned from past experiences that men tend to hold out information from women if they think the women are interested. Crazy game, this battle of love, but it's true.

"Private until you're ready to get serious."

"Serious about what?"

"Behaving."

"Ah," I sighed. We'd had this little discussion before. Marcus firmly believed that I could very much use a bit of discipline in my world. He felt that although I had my life in basic order, and from the outside most people were convinced that I had my shit together, my inattention to details was due to a lack of focus. Discipline, he insisted would help me rise to a higher level, help me to succeed in my artistic career as well as in my private life. How did I feel about all that? I just wasn't sure. Basically, it sounded too serious for a free spirit such as myself. "Serious" was exactly the word Marcus favored, even though I cringed at the term.

"I won't rush you," he assured me. "We'll move at your pace."

My pace, I thought. I didn't have any idea what "my pace" might be. This whole concept was entirely alien to me. Behaving because a lover commanded it? That struck a chord inside me, but I didn't know why. In the past, the kinkiest thing I'd ever done was to engage in anal sex. And that was after a great deal of coaxing and with a veritable ocean of lubricant. Yes, I'd enjoyed it, but the act wasn't something on my everyday menu. Now, my beau was asking me to change my world entirely. To put myself in his hands—he would be my Master, "Master with a capital *M*," he explained repeatedly—and I would be his slave. Lowercase *s*, of course.

He didn't expect me to quit my day job at the gallery, nor to walk on the end of a leash in public or disappear into some frightening old-fashioned dungeon setting where I'd be chained naked to a wall, fed bread and water when I was lucky, and be expected to lick his feet at any moment of the day. But at home, in the privacy of his quarters, he wanted me to obey. That was a big word for me. Christ, I couldn't even obey my own inner commands; how on earth was I supposed to behave for Marcus?

"You're not," he promised. "That's the whole thing. If you could do that, I'd have no use for you, Melissa. Obedience is what I will teach you. Eventually, you will learn to *want* to obey. And then your entire world will change. I know you've got it inside of you to be—"

"The best I can be?" I shot back, smart-aleck style.

"That's the ARMY," he sighed, "and no, that sort of response won't go over big with me. That would have earned you a quick spanking that would have brought tears to your eyes."

At the word "spanking," I tried to laugh but found that I couldn't even manage a giggle. Spanking. Why did the concept make me wetter than wet? Why did I squirm in my seat and try to distract Marcus from the gist of what he was trying to say?

"If you'd let me finish," he continued in his calm, careful way of speaking, "I'd have said that you've got it in yourself to be sublime rather than scattered, to be cool and self-contained rather than frantic and frustrated."

All of that sounded good to me, but I couldn't help being my usual cocky self anyway. "What do I call you?" I muttered, sounded like a pouty teenager. "You don't really want me to refer to you as Master, do you? What about Daddy? Or Mr. King?"

"*Sir* will do nicely," he said, sending a new shiver through me, one that made me pause and really consider the offer for the first time. *Seriously* consider it, to use his pet word. As I said, for some strange reason, the concept of being spanked by Marcus had made me instantaneously wet. Besides, my rationalization continued, wasn't I tired of buying books called *Zen and the Art of Any Fucking Thing*? Tired of drinking wheat grass and juice and going to predawn yoga classes in order to find a "center" I wasn't entirely sure existed within my lithe form. More important than all of that, I liked him. A lot. If things didn't go well, I could always bail. That's my M.O. Get going when the going gets rocky, turbulent, disturbing, or distracting. Marcus said he doubted I'd ever want to leave. That if he knew me the way he thought he did, I'd be his forever.

And then he took me to the Counting House.

It was a bit like being marched out behind the shed as a naughty kid. My knees felt just as weak, and my stomach did flip-flops, because suddenly I knew—don't ask how, I just did—that the Counting House wasn't a place where Marcus King counted his coins. It wasn't his secret hideaway where he dressed in a loose ecru-hued caftan, placed a padded mat in the center of the room, and said "Ohm" to the background music of splashing computer-generated waterfalls. No, this was a place where I was going to pay for my infractions to his detailed rules and regulations, and I was going to pay with my own skin.

As soon as he opened the door, I felt reassured. He hadn't taken me to a frightening place at all. No cold stone walls. No heavy chains. The floor was painted a deep cobalt blue that gleamed as if the paint was still wet, and the entire room was empty save for an odd contraption made of wood covered with cardinal-red leather pads, a large black wardrobe, and a mattress covered in what looked like a neoprene sheet.

"Take off your shoes," Marcus told me. Quickly, I kicked off my mules. "Now, take off everything else." With my eyes focused on the shut-and-locked wardrobe, I undressed. Marcus observed me in his careful manner, and then he started lighting candles around the room. When the entire place glowed brightly, he turned off the overhead light. "Are you ready?" he asked.

I nodded.

"Then walk to the horse and bend over it."

Again, I obeyed his command as fast as I could, and I realized that I was trying my best to show him what an obedient person I could be. But even as I felt him binding me into place, I knew that my actions were lies to the both of us. He wanted my head to be clear, my only thoughts of obedience. But there was a racket in my skull that I could not silence. Words ricocheted around in my brain: fear, reprisals, disobedience, anger, confusion, the possibility of pain. . . . And then suddenly, magically, my mental conversations began to dissipate as Marcus walked toward the wardrobe and unlocked the padlock. The door swung open only wide enough for me to catch a tiny glimpse of what lay hidden inside, but the few items I did see—a bamboo cane, a crop, something that looked like a cat-o'-nine-tails made of purple suede—sent pure shivers through me.

Marcus withdrew a simple wooden paddle, the type used for playing Ping-Pong, and shut the door. He came to my side and placed the paddle against my naked ass.

"Count for me, Melissa," Marcus insisted. "You count every stroke."

Ah, I got it as he said the words: The Counting House. But understanding the concept didn't make the pain any easier to accept. Even before he brought the paddle down in the first blow, my body twisted to get out of the way. What was I doing here? Why had I agreed to this?

"Remember your safe word," Marcus whispered to me.

"Yes," I nodded. I remembered.

"Use it at any time," he told me, "but use it only when you need to."

Now, I needed to *now*. I didn't really want this, did I? Wasn't ready for this sort of deal, this type of situation—

Again, the words were silenced in my head, this time by the sensation of the paddle meeting my ass. The connection of the textured paddle against my ripe, ready hindquarters made a loud, cracking sound. I heard it before I felt it, and I'd received a second blow before I actually had absorbed the first one, and also before I'd been able to say the word "One."

"Count," Marcus reminded me. "Each time you forget, we start back at the beginning."

So those two didn't add up in the larger scheme of things. Immediately, I understood the game. Biting into the fullness of my bottom lip, I assured myself that I wouldn't let myself—or Marcus—down again. My ass throbbed already, but for some strange and unexplainable reason, I didn't want the pain to stop. It was like the feeling of working out with a trainer at the gym, pushing myself to surpass previous limits, to make him proud of my accomplishments. Now, I wanted to prove something to Marcus, something I'd only be able to prove if he continued my punishment.

"One," I said this time as he struck a blow on my right cheek. Then "two" as a matching blow landed on my left. I could feel that my pussy had awoken during this entire encounter, and I wondered if Marcus knew that, if he understood how wet I'd become already —probably from the first step into this strange and inexplicably beautiful room. "Three," I murmured as he continued the punishment, and then the blows became faster, raining down on me, and I understood he was trying to make me fail. If I lost track, or lost myself in the pain and odd, mind-numbing pleasure of the spanking, than he'd begin at one again. And just as I had that thought, I realized that I had no idea what number we were on. "Seven?" I tried, hesitantly.

"No, Melissa," he said, "we're back to one—" and he struck again. My ass felt swollen already, bigger than normal, pulsating with heat. And my pussy—my drenched pussy—was leaking sweet sex juices down my thighs. Christ, was I on two now? Or four? I threw my head back and guessed, "Three?"

"One," Marcus snapped. "We're back to one."

I felt tears welling up in my eyes. Would this game go all night? How scarlet red would my ass actually have to be before he stopped? For a second, Marcus hesitated, bending down on his knees and cradling my face in his hands. "You're trying to be good, aren't you?"

I nodded.

"That's half the trick," he said. "Pay attention. Focus only on me. On what I want. Quiet those random, fluttering thoughts in your head. Pay attention—"

And then he was behind me again, but this time, I felt something else against my naked rear. He had his cock out, was probing between my thighs, and I sighed loudly at the satisfaction of feeling him start to fuck me. That sigh turned into a groan when I felt the paddle pressed against my right flank. What could he possibly do now?

Spank me as he fucked me. That became clear in only a moment. I lowered my head, resigned, and numbered the blows that accompanied the strokes of his rigid cock. The numbers were a mantra, a mesmerizing cadence that took me slowly to a place I'd never been. I felt the pleasure build within me, and I pressed my hips hard against the horse, gaining contact with the smooth shiny red leather against my naked clit. I rubbed fiercely as Marcus continued to both spank and fuck me, and when I felt myself coming, I still was able to count.

Don't know how.

Don't know why.

But I understood as the pleasure beat through me exactly what the Counting House was for, and why I might so crave to visit it again—and often—in the future.

CCCCO

Lucky Number Seven

⟐ BY G. LIPTON ⟐

EGAS.

It's a one-word town. Say the name, and people instantly conjure up images. Neon. Flashing lights. Jangling coins. Throngs of people. Flashy cars. Flashier outfits. Easy money. Easy sex. Vegas.

It's almost an adjective. "God, she was so fucking 'Vegas,' I couldn't handle her." Hear that statement, and you'd know in a minute the girl had fake boobs and a shitload of faux blonde hair and an inhuman tan from either a bottle or a bed—or both. "Vegas Guys" are equally as unbearable. The ones with the dark curly chest hair and the rippling pecs all look as if they're from a casting call for boys named "Guido." The ones just out to cruise the strip have a younger, tousled air to them, but you know they'll be brittle and bruised in no time. They live to hit the bars. To party with girls who are more than ready to take their clothes off—if they haven't done so already.

I see it all. In fact, I see way too much of it all. The cleavage from a canister of silicone and the blowjobs delivered off in a corner when nobody thinks you're watching.

The passes made and missed, made and received. The money, so much easy money, flowing through people's fingertips like meaningless strips of paper confetti. In Vegas, money doesn't have the same power as in normal places. Vegas money is vacation money—didn't think you'd go home with it anyway, so why not feed it to a one-armed bandit. Close your eyes, take a spin, press your luck, you might win.

Might.

I work security, and I'm thankfully at the point in my career where I can watch the goings-on from behind the scenes without getting personally involved. Don't need to be down on the floor in the casino anymore. Don't need to smell the smells of too much perfume and cologne, forever recycling in the constantly circulating air. Maybe I'm a bit jaded now. I used to live for the excitement of being in the thick of things. Today, I'm content to kick back and watch. Watch and critique.

"You're all cold," my partner Stan said once. "You don't get a hard-on for any of the girls anymore."

He was scoping out a bunch of showgirls on his screen, ranking them in the order that he'd most like to fuck them.

"They don't do anything for me," I said.

"That's because you're cold. You don't have a heart anymore. You don't believe that fantasies really can come true."

"You're right," I told him. "Not in Vegas." I scanned the bank of screens, satisfied to be doing my job, because watching has always been what I do best.

Which is how she caught my eye so quickly. She wasn't Vegas. Not in the slightest. Not in the true definition of the word. She was—well, don't know precisely. I guess you'd have to say that she was the opposite of Vegas. White to Vegas's dirty black hole of a heart.

"Look at *her*," Stan said, whistling through his teeth. "Just look at her, for fuck's sake. You know what I'm saying, right? Look at her."

Even on the black-and-white screen, she was mesmerizing. There was an innocent quality to her that I found undeniably fetching, and yet as I continued to watch, I thought I saw something cunning in those dark eyes. She knew precisely how amazing she looked, even if the overall attitude she portrayed was one of infinite effortlessness.

"Going on a break," I told Stan, "be back in ten."

Honestly, I needed to see her in person. Didn't need to tell that to Stan, though. He'd have ribbed me about it until the next millennium. Yeah, she'd stunned me on the TV screen, but there's nothing like real life to show a person's flaws. Not that I wouldn't have been interested even if I found a few flaws. Flaws are real. Flaws aren't Vegas at all. Still, I was yearning to see what she looked like outside of a television screen. I wanted to watch her breathe.

I found her easily enough at the craps table, surrounded by six guys, rolling the dice like a pro. And the truth be told, there were no flaws in sight.

Instead of gleaming white-blonde hair, hers was so black it shone with a hypnotic blue light. Instead of bottle-bronzed, her skin was the palest, creamy white. Ethereal pale, almost translucent. Except for her cheeks, which were a perfect rose. I watched her shake the dice in her hand and let them fly, and I saw from the stack of chips on the table that she was winning. And big. When I took my eyes off her for a moment, I realized there was something odd about her group of fellow gamblers. They were all sort

of shortish guys, with graying beards, the red noses of serious drinkers, and a habit of referring to each other as
"Happy" and "Sleepy." As in, "Hey, Sleepy, she's killing
you. Look'it Snow go!"

"Shut up, Happy—"

I shook my head. This was too strange.

Snow White and the Seven—

Uh oh, that wasn't right. I tallied the motley crew again.
There were six. Not seven. I was so taken by the strange
sight, that I actually said those words out loud, and the
lovely Snow looked my way, even thought I'd spoken in a
whisper. She gave me what I can only describe as a deeply
encouraging glance, and then set down the dice and moved
to my side.

"You said 'six.' "

It wasn't a question, but I nodded anyway.

"I'm short one tonight," she continued. "Grumpy
couldn't make it."

Now I smiled. Her eyes looked me up and down. "You
don't fit as his replacement," she said, "but I guess you'll
have to do."

"Do you mean that I'm not short enough, not drunk
enough, or not surly enough?"

"You're perfect," she said, and then she waved to the
men, who were already back to gambling, and led me to
the bank of elevators, then up to her room.

She was in a suite, and although I know the run of the
hotel, this one had passed by me somehow. We have some
pretty wild rooms in the joint, suites with eight-foot-tall
champagne glass whirlpools. Water beds. Beds that play
music. Beds that vibrate. But this room beat them all. The
decor was what I'd call "Woodland Spirit," with rich green

leaves in velvet-flocked wallpaper, and a babbling brook of a waterfall cascading into a hot tub in the center of the room. I thought I even heard the sound of birds cooing, but I couldn't waste my time looking, because Snow was beckoning me into the tub.

Man, did she look good. Her skin took on a rosier glow instantly as she lowered herself into the steaming bath. She had no false modesty, simply posed naked in the bubbling water and cocked her head in my direction. What was I waiting for? That's the question I saw in her eyes. What *was* I waiting for? Christ, nothing. I joined her in a second, kicking out of my clothes faster than I ever have before. I didn't want this vision to evaporate.

In the water, she came into my arms and settled herself astride my lap. Sweet Snow knew exactly what she was doing. I felt her body move on me, and I realized that she didn't want me to do anything. This wasn't a girl waiting for her prince to come and bring her to passionate climax. She was the one working me, pushing her body up and back, gaining control of the ride. I let her. I would have let her do anything. She felt so good, the whole action was amazing. With the bubbles of the water, the turbulence all around us, it was like fucking in some enchanted hot springs. All the more enchanted because of how stunning the woman looked, her hair curling slightly in the moist heat, her body sleekly feline in some places, fully rounded in others.

My cock slid easily inside of her, and I could feel her muscles tightening on me. Oh, did she know a thing or seven about bringing a man pleasure. I couldn't remember the last time I'd been with a girl who really moved me. Now all I wanted to do was cradle her face in my hands, to kiss her, to bite her full bottom lip as I thrusted inside of her.

As I started to come, she whispered, "So glad the show got canceled tonight—"

"Canceled?" I murmured, confused and coming and out of my head.

"Our understudy was out sick, and you just can't put on a show without all seven of the dwarfs!" and suddenly everything started to make more sense. I realized that she was Snow White from the Snow White Ice Show down the street, and that maybe she was missing Grumpy tonight, but he was just some short actor who caused trouble for the show's producer.

But none of that was important to me, because I knew who I was, and that was all that mattered: Lucky number seven. Sometimes fairy tale fantasies do come true.

Even in Vegas.

Mistress, to You

❧ BY DANTE DAVIDSON ❧

HERE was an old woman—okay she wasn't really that old. She was "older," but very hot. Older in the exact same way that Jerry Hall is older, or the way Isabella Rossellini is older, if you catch my drift. I mean, you wouldn't turn either of those beauties out of your bed, would you? No way.

So this stunning, mature woman, with a fantastically fit body and a cascade of silver-streaked coal-black hair, lived in a shoe. Well, not precisely a shoe, of course. A shoe-shaped house, if you were looking at it from above, like in a helicopter, or something. Boot-shaped, really, with a longer portion and a shorter portion. Christ, maybe it was more like an L. I don't know a hell of a lot about houses. Architecture's not my specialty. Ask me about something I *do* know about, like kinky sex. Or dungeons. Or administering discipline to naughty lovers.

Anyway, back to my story. This woman didn't have any children. That wasn't her problem at all. Wasn't like she missed the chance—she'd just never wanted any. What she did have was a plethora of lovers who *acted* like children. Bad little "boys" and "girls"—grown-ups, of course, but naughty fucking grown-ups, you know the type—who craved to submit to the power of her awesome authority. They needed more than that, if truth be told. They needed the stinging feeling of her hand delivering well-earned spankings, the serious crack of a crop against their naked behinds. They needed to be bound in place by her expensive black stockings, to be cuffed by their wrists or suspended using heavy-duty ropes. And when they were really and truly naughty, they needed much more than that. They needed all sorts of deviant escapist activities: risqué role-playing games, erotic enemas, public humiliation.

She was good, this woman. She understood precisely when it was time to lead one of her lovers down the long boot-shaped hallway to her bedroom, to lock the door behind her, and to spank that naughty miscreant until his or her bottom was decidedly red. (Didn't matter to her whether the person was male or female. Sex to her was sex.) She knew what to do after the spanking, as well, what to do with various sex toys and lubricants and vibrating wands. . . .

So to backtrack a little bit, there was this mature and stunning woman, with a whole sumptuous dark mane of that rich, long, silver-streaked hair, who lived in an L-shaped mansion on the outskirts of Beverly Hills, and who was such a fucking good dominatrix she had far too many clients to care for. So what she did was place an ad in the *Los Angeles Weekly* for assistance—and that's where I entered the picture.

My name's Adam. Good to fucking meet you.

The ad was simple enough. Said that a clean, well-respected fantasy haven for consenting adults of considerable means was currently hiring for a male dominant. Said that looks were far more important than experience and that a positive attitude and a willingness to learn was a must. I'm comfortable with myself enough to have answered the ad without a problem. I'm tall, strong, and lean, with long dark hair and the type of green eyes that all women tend to fall for. I've handled my share of naughty lovers for my own personal pleasure. Nothing sexier than delivering an OTK spanking on a well-deserving little ass before engaging in a ferocious back-door romp. Doing it for pay was an idea that gave me a rock-solid hard-on. Could I turn a nubile young thing over my lap and paddle her bottom for her? You bet. Could I do all that was required for the job without falling in love or getting tangled up in any emotional strings? That's what Mistress Catherine wanted to know. I thought I could. I thought that taking care of people's fantasies would be thrilling enough, that I wouldn't find myself emotionally involved—

But that didn't work exactly as I had planned.

Not that I fell for one of my clients. Oh, no. Not that. After years of living the L.A. lifestyle, my heart has grown far too cold for that. But I fell for *her*. Fell hard for Mistress Catherine herself. She of the icy countenance and unreadable expressions. It happened to me in a heartbeat. First, I was fine with my station in life, working nights, spending all that extra cash on any frivolity that caught my eye, then I was conflicted to the point where I didn't think I could get out of bed and go to work. Not without her knowing immediately what was wrong with me.

I didn't know what to do. But finally I decided I'd simply quit. Tell her that the work wasn't what I'd expected, that I was going back to my previous job, slaving behind the bar at one of the hard rock clubs in Hollywood.

She eyed me carefully when I walked into her office to confess. Actually, confessing wasn't what I meant to do. I meant to clearly state the fact that this would be my last day. Yeah, I liked the money a lot, and I liked getting off on the job, a daily experience. Liked paddling the pretty red-heads and bleach-blondes, and bottle-black beauties who weren't getting what they needed from their lovers at home. Liked wielding a whip in front of a crowd and making the audience, and the slave bound before me, beg for more. Oh, Adam, more!

Didn't change the way I felt about Catherine, and that's why I was giving her my resignation.

She wouldn't take it.

"Excuse me?"

"Can't leave. You're too fucking good. It's in your blood. I'm not letting you leave until you tell me the real reason."

I was silent.

"Because," she continued, "I can smell the lie on you."

So I stood there, in her well-appointed office, and I shook my head. I couldn't say it. I saw the way she demolished weaker people. I wouldn't be one of them. No way. No how. I stared down at my motorcycle boots, and I felt like a naughty schoolkid, stammering in front of the headmistress. What could I say to make her let me go? What could I possibly say to convince her that what I really wanted was to be away from her, when that was the furthest thing from the truth imaginable.

"I read people well, Adam," Catherine said softly. "That's why I'm so good at my job. You have the same skill. I'd never seen it in another employee. Not before you. But here's the trick—you can't always read the needs in yourself."

Now, what the fuck did that mean? And why was Catherine walking toward me with that purposeful stride, a look in her dark brown eyes that I couldn't immediately decipher? And why was she leading me—me!—out the door of her office and down that long narrow hallway to the master suite, the bedroom reserved for only the highest-paying clientele.

Oh, Christ, I shook my head. I was too easy for her. She saw through me so well, binding me neatly down on the bed in the center of the room, removing the various tools and toys, implements of destruction and desire. I closed my eyes and held my breath as she prepared me for what I knew would be an unforgettable experience. Then she was up on the bed with me, her lips pressed to my ear as she whispered her plans. Each and every thing she was going to do to me that evening. I shuddered as she spoke, and when she was finished, she said, "Can you do it without the ties?"

I nodded.

"That's not the way you answer your mistress."

"Yes," I said immediately. "Yes, Mistress Catherine."

She liked the way I spoke to her. I could tell. "Good boy," she said, stroking her delicate fingers through my hair, "Such a good boy," she said before she undid the bondage, then slipped the harness around her hips and prepared to fuck me.

"Hold yourself open for me," she insisted.

Dumbly, I reached back to part the cheeks of my ass.

"Wider," she insisted and I scrambled to please her.

The humiliation in this action flooded through me, as did the knowledge that being taken like this was going to make me come. I felt the cold swish of lube from her fingertips to my asshole, and then I felt the head of the dildo thrust its way inside of me. My breathing grew instantly quicker, and I thanked Catherine mentally for trusting me enough not to bind me down. There was a strength in submitting to her power, in holding myself still for the brutal force behind her thrusts. She knew. She always reads her clients right.

And that's why there is now not just an old woman in that shoe, but a young man at her side, one who's never going to leave.

Not fucking ever.

CCCCO

Never Talk to Strangers

⌐ BY CHERIE McINTOSH ⌐

NCE upon a time in La-La Land, there lived a mesmerizing girl who was as beautiful as she was kindhearted. This delicate creature was indeed a rare find, especially because she lived in the Hollywood Hills where there are plenty of people with beauty on the outside (thanks to Botox, plastic surgery, and power yoga), but not nearly enough with beauty within.

Due to a series of unfortunate circumstances, this lovely lady found herself rooming with her stepmother and stepsister, both of whom could have used healthy dosages of Prozac to make their torrid tempers more even. The girl did all of the housework, the dishes, the laundry, and any unpleasant task her relations could conceive of—yet although she was heaped in drudgery, she never complained. While her stepmother and stepsister bemoaned the evils of the day, the girl kept a smile on her face. When they wailed about how nothing was sacred, how it wasn't safe to go outdoors, or especially to talk to strangers, the girl simply tilted her head and smiled her kind smile.

She didn't agree with the advice, but she never let on.

The thing was that she *liked* to talk to strangers—one stranger in specific, the man who delivered their bottled water every week. He was a stranger she couldn't get out of her head. He had shaggy blond hair and a surfer's tan, and he was always ready with a positive word, even if he was only commenting about the weather.

The girl's stepsister and mother refused to even look at the boy, feeling themselves well above his stature in life, but the girl always made sure she was home at the designated delivery hour. She liked the way he looked at her, the way he didn't rush to get back to his truck and on to his next appointment. Once, he'd almost kissed her—she was sure of it—but her stepmother had entered the kitchen at precisely that moment, squelching any romantic possibilities with her dour arrival.

Since that day, the girl spent hours fantasizing about the man, his smooth skin, his dark blue eyes, the way he seemed to devour her with his gaze when she walked to open the door for him. What his large hands might feel like around her waist, she wondered. What his broad chest might look like if he peeled off his T-shirt and then admired him, standing there half-naked before her. Sometimes, late at night, she thought about more than looking at him in a state of undress. She thought about kissing along his chest in a line, moving south with each press of her lips to his bare skin. She thought about coming to the middle of his body, opening her mouth and drawing him in. His cock, that is. Drawing his long, hard cock down her throat, swallowing on him and seeing if she could make him moan and arch his handsome body upward on the bed. She'd heard talk of what happened after that, about the eruption that would occur in a man when he reached his finishing point.

The thought of drinking down the juices from his own body made her so lustfully thirsty she could hardly stand it.

Where these thoughts came from, she didn't know, but every time she had one of these sort of fantasies, she found that she had to touch herself between her legs, to rub and rub until the mysterious feeling passed in shades of multi-colored pleasure that left her breathless, yet selfishly craving more.

One afternoon, her evil stepmother demanded that the girl head down to the well in the back of their property and bring back a pitcher of water.

"The water delivery boy will be here shortly," the girl reminded her, wishing for a few moments by herself so that she could pretty herself up for her dream man.

"I've got a hankering for fresh water," the stepmother insisted.

With a sweet shrug, the girl headed down the steep slope to the well. When she arrived, she saw an elderly woman straining for a drink. Without a thought, the girl dropped to her knees and fetched the old woman a cup of the water. The woman thanked the girl and then said, "You are as kind as you are lovely, and I wish to bestow upon you a gift."

"De nada," the girl smiled.

"Whenever you speak," the woman said, "diamonds and flowers and other jewels will fall from your lips."

"Oh, no," the girl said, startled as rubies and emeralds spilled free. "That's no good at all. People will think I'm a freak show!"

The woman started back, surprised that her wish hadn't pleased the girl. "Then what would you like?"

"Truly?"

The old lady nodded, for she was indeed a fairy, and didn't mind shifting wishes to suit the needs of the people she chose to so cleverly surprise.

"There's this boy—" the girl said.

"Ah," the fairy nodded. "A boy."

"And I just adore him."

"Who is he?"

"The water man. He's so sexy and handsome, and I'm dying for him to ask me out. To *seek* me out—"

The woman thought for a moment and then said, "I can give you another gift of oral pleasures, if you'd rather. Once this man has one moment between your lips, he will never look at another girl."

Now the young woman's eyes brightened, and she nodded.

"Take those as well," the old fairy instructed, pointing to the gems that had fallen from the girl's lips already. "Although they're not as much as you might have had if you'd kept that gift of mine, they'll definitely set you up nicely for the rest of your days. And, I'm afraid to say, you'll continue to spill jewels and flowers from your lips until midnight tonight. That's the shortest spell I can cast."

The girl quickly scooped up the jewels and headed up to the house. Once there, she was accosted by her stepmother. "What took you so long?" the stepmother demanded in her characteristically acidic way.

"Oh, nothing," the girl said, but as she spoke diamonds, roses, tourmalines, and other lovely creations dropped to the floor.

"Nothing, my ass," her stepmother shrieked and she forced the girl to tell the whole story, watching wide-eyed as the jewels piled up around the two of them. When she fully understood the fairy tale that the girl had told, the stepmother called for her own hideous daughter into the room.

"Get your lazy self down to the well," she demanded, "and wait for an old hag. Grant her every wish, and she will make us rich."

While this was going on, the young lovely girl packed her bags in the spare room, singing quietly to herself and gathering up each gem as it fell. She stayed only long enough to hear what happened when the troll of a sister showed up. As her evil sister spoke, toads and snakes spilled from her mouth. "This beautiful woman met me at the well and demanded a cup of water. I told her to get it herself. What did I look like? A bar wench? And *this* is what happened—" Geckos and lizards littered the floor by the end of her tale. "Even worse, mother, she cursed me so that if ever I give a man a blowjob, he will howl and screech in pain."

Laughing softly to herself, the pretty sister exited the house, awaiting the arrival of the delivery man—who had no idea what good luck awaited him!

Once Upon a Time

⊰ BY ANN BLAKELY ⊱

EOPLE always want the "happily ever after." They wait for it, sitting upright, breaths held, desperate for the part of the fairy tale in which some cookie-cutter Prince Charming and a bland Princess No-Name find themselves all dolled up in blindingly clichéd wedding gear, committing to a loser's lifetime of brainless bliss. The concept works well for the masses, and that's fine. Who am I to judge?

But for me, the thrill is strictly in the "once upon a time." I guess that makes me sort of a slut. In my defense, let me explain. By the time you've reached "happily ever after," you know everything there is to know about your mate. How he likes to sleep. What he wears to bed. Who he hangs out with on his day off. You know his ATM code, which war movies he has memorized, his favorite color, food, and Beatle—and sure, that sort of awesome intimacy can be great. But in my opinion, it can also be pretty damn boring. I mean, who really cares about which side of the bed he favors, or what brand of toothpaste his mother always bought, or why he has an innate fear of roller-coaster rides? None of that can make a girl wet. None of that is as powerful as "once upon a time."

Don't believe me? Then check this out:

Once upon a time, I kissed a handsome waiter upstairs at a chic Manhattan restaurant while my date thought I was innocently making a phone call. The waiter, who had been softly flirting with me all through dinner, pressed me up against the wall so that I could feel how hard he was, and he wrapped my hair around his fist as he kissed me. I knew exactly what it would be like to fuck him, the ruthless intensity of his thrusts, the way I'd ache all over afterward. We made out until my lips felt bruised, my legs felt weak, and I could hardly remember my date's name when I shakily made my way back downstairs.

Or . . .

Once upon a time, a coworker brushed up against me in the coffee room, and I thought I might actually come on the spot when he bent to whisper in my ear that all he wanted to do was put me over his lap and give me a spanking. A thorough spanking, one that a bad girl like me really needed. Deserved, even. He said that he'd been thinking about doing just that since the very first time I strutted past his office in my short red miniskirt. As he spoke, he cradled and caressed my ass, and I thought that he might actually make the scene come true, might truly spank my naked ass in the coffee room while our coworkers moved down the hall, oblivious to what was happening mere feet away.

Or . . .

Once upon a time, I found myself standing at a pay phone on University Avenue, calling a lover I had no right to call, telling him secrets I had no right to possess. Telling him that if I could get away for an hour later on in the evening, I'd drive to his apartment so that he could fuck me, sodomize me, come all over me. Telling him that was all I had thought about all day long, his cock in my ass, his come on my skin.

All of those scenarios are sexier to me than any self-righteous happily ever after. And that's why I said I'm sort of a slut, because if you crave the magic of the start of a relationship, then you also crave the freedom of the end, the thrill of the moving on to the next one.

I know there are many tried-and-true ways to "keep the spark alive" in long-term situations. Games you can play. Mental tricks to enliven a dull situation. But I never bother. I need the kissing in the back room, the groping in the elevator, the up-all-night fuck sessions that fade when you move in. Don't know why. They just do. Seems to me that if you find someone you're compatible with, sexually and emotionally, then the sex should only get better. The excitement should only grow. But I haven't ever found that yet—

"Because you don't stick around long enough," Brock told me after listening to my theory of love in the year 2000.

"What?"

"You have to give a relationship time before you flee. Then you can see if the sex will get better or worse, if the excitement will grow or fade away."

Spoken like a true bartender. One who's seen it all. When I voiced *that* opinion, he just grinned.

"Not 'it all,' " he said, "but I've seen you, and how you operate. You're like a fucking gazelle, the way you prance away as soon as the dust starts to settle."

"Or as soon as the lions arrive," I sneered, annoyed. Nobody likes to hear their lives so easily summed up. And I always envisioned myself more like a panther than a goddamn gazelle. And when I said *that,* Brock laughed out loud. "Panthers don't spook the way you do."

"Spook. Spooked of what?"

"Getting real. Growing up."

"I don't want to grow up," I said smugly. "I don't need seriousness in my life."

"You don't know shit about serious," Brock said, and moved down the bar to serve someone else.

Was he right? Did I not know? Had I never bothered to learn? I waited for Brock to return to his spot in front of my bar stool, and when he finally did, I said, "So teach me."

"You don't have it in you to be my pupil."

My arousal was piqued. Brock's handsome. Movie-star handsome. Which is why I always think it's so cool that he likes being a bartender, that he has no aspirations of moving to Hollyweird and joining the millions of other hopefuls who are as good-looking as he is. With his chiseled features, dark eyes, black hair, he looks part Superman, part Latin lover.

"Try me," I said, and I wondered why my voice trembled when I spoke those simple words.

"You can't flee," he said. "You can't spook and leave a cloud of dust as you kick up your heels in those Manolos of yours."

"And you can't bore me," I told him. "That's a simple enough deal, isn't it? We don't need to get the lawyers involved, right?"

He smiled his standard half-smile at me, then slid a key in my direction. "You meet me at my apartment," he instructed, giving me the address and access code. "I'll be there in three hours. I want you naked, in the middle of my bed, and I don't want you to have come. Not until I get there. Leave that part to me."

All I could think of as I drove to his place was the once-upon-a-time thrill coursing through me proved my argument precisely. That and the fact that all I wanted to do was touch myself until I came. Oh, I could imagine it easily, my fingers probing through my turquoise satin panties at first, working around and around my clit until I couldn't stand it any longer and needed the direct contact of skin to skin.

Why was I so desperate to get myself off? Because he'd told me not to. Who was he to tell me anything? He was my bartender. How nuts was that? But there was more to our connection. I'd always gone out of my way to tell him in great detail about my most fabulous encounters, hoping to get a rise out of him, some sort of change of expression that would let me know he heard, that he was envisioning me doing the things that I told him, that he might be envisioning doing those same things with me.

At his apartment, I found myself following his stated rules—doing exactly what he'd told me to. The excitement bubbled through me, and I wondered whether he *would* be able to keep up the intensity. If he could, then maybe, just maybe I'd met my match.

When Brock got home, I was naked in the middle of his bed, and my pussy was so swollen and hungry that I thought I might come from him looking at me. Luckily, we didn't wait to see if that was a scientific possibility. Brock gruffly said, "Good girl," and then pulled me toward him, not even bothering to take off his own clothes. He pressed his face against my naked pussy and began to lick up and down over my clit until I was nearly out of my head with desire. He was good. Amazing, even. He knew the little tricks that only men who genuinely like to go down on girls know about. He knew to trace letters or figure eights or designs or *something* over and over, to alternate the pressure, to give me a breather when I thought I was going to implode or explode—to dissolve into white hot shimmers of iridescent light.

He used one hand to gently finger-fuck my pussy, crossing his middle finger over his pointer to fill me up further. I squeezed down against him, letting him know how hot I was, and how close to coming.

"See?" he murmured against my skin. "Good girls are rewarded when they listen to their lovers—" His voice and his tongue and his whisper-soft whiskers tickled against my skin, and just as he finished speaking, I came, my hips bucking against him, my whole body alive. But I couldn't silence the thought in my head.

"And bad girls?" I murmured, desperate. "What about bad girls?"

"Ah," he said, making me shiver with his smile. "You try me out. You test me and I'll let you find out for yourself all about what happens to bad girls."

We spent the night making love, topsy-turvy love. And the next day, and the next. And the next week, and month, and year. And it never got old. Hasn't to this day. Brock always has some way to keep my interest alive, some sparkling method, some suggestion for me to try not to break, if I want him to take care of me the way he knows I do—

Because I do. I really do. I want him to take care of me

Brock-style. For now and forever. And so here I am, a once-upon-a-time girl, deeply serious about a happily-ever-after boy. But tonight, as I test the handcuffs to see if there's any give, I know deep in myself that this is not your ordinary sort of fairy tale.

CCCCO

The Princess and the Penis

⊰ BY RONALD KELLER ⊱

LANTED shafts of light streamed through the open curtains, bathing the king-size bed in warm sunlight. Sprawled out in the light with the covers tossed to one side, Princess slumbered, the bright shafts turning her filmy silk nightshirt into a translucent veil, shrouding her tempting curves. It was eight o'clock on a Sunday, the morning after our first date. We had made love late into the morning, and now Princess lay exhausted.

Her real name was Carolyn, but I preferred to think of her by the name she used to post on the Sleepy Beauties Web site. "Princess."

I nuzzled up against her, remembering the tender moments we'd shared the night before. My cock started to harden.

Princess and I had chatted online for months before discovering that we lived in the same city. By then, Princess had confessed all her fondest erotic dreams, and they had one thing in common.

"My favorite fantasy is to be made love to while sleeping, and not to be awakened," she'd told me in an e-mail early on in our interaction. "I'm a very deep sleeper," she'd added. "But no one's ever been able to do it."

Now, I nudged my lips up against her ear and whispered softly, "Princess?"

She sighed gently in her slumber. Her eyes flickered suggestively under their lids. I wondered what she was dreaming.

She lay on her back. Her breasts strained through the thin material of her nightie, nipples erect. Whatever she was dreaming, I was quite sure it was interesting.

I ran my fingertips over her breasts, caressing the curve of her thighs and touching her pussy through her filmy string panties. I moved slowly, careful not to upset the bed. I tugged her panties down over her smooth ass, drawing them away from her pussy, still moist with last night's reverie. I eased her panties down her thighs, over her calves. I slipped them over her ankles and tossed them away.

"Princess?" I whispered.

She didn't make a move. She really *was* a very deep sleeper.

I eased her legs open and slid, naked, on top of her. I began to nuzzle her ear, whispering "This is for you" as I nudged the entrance of her pussy with the head of my cock. It was slick with arousal and opened wide for me. She gasped as the head entered her; I paused as her mouth worked in somnambulant mumbles and then her eyes went back to rolling in their REM-sleep dance. With a slow thrust, I entered her all the way, and a tiny, sleepy sigh escaped her lips.

Her pussy embraced me, wet and tender. I started to

slide gently in and out of her, my hands gently caressing her breasts through silk. She moaned in her sleep, but didn't say a word. I entered her rhythmically in slow, savoring thrusts, loving the way her pussy reacted to me while her eyes continued their midnight fandango. I kissed her slightly parted lips; they remained slack, loose, motionless.

A tiny whimper rumbled through her throat, as her hips began to pulse in response to my thrusts. I said her name again. "Princess?"

She lay still and did not respond.

With a few more thrusts, however, her hips began to grind, her body taking over while her mind was disengaged. She started to thrash in her sleep, clawing the bed as she writhed under me. I was almost on the edge of my own orgasm when I realized Princess was going to come.

"I can have orgasms in my sleep," she'd told me in an early e-mail. "I guess they're like wet dreams."

This dream was definitely wet—soaking. Her pussy, tight around my cock, was moistening further as her sleeping body strove toward orgasm. When she began to shudder, I felt the spasms of her pussy around my cock, gripping me in a tender embrace as she came. Her lips parted wide and her breath came out in a rapturous moan. All the while, her eyes continued to move.

I came, my cock seized by the ecstasy of her pussy's embrace. I moaned and kissed her sleeping lips, not even caring anymore if I awakened her. But she remained still, now, sleeping. Her eyes had paused their movements.

I lay atop her and sank back into exhaustion, loving the feel of her body curled against me.

It was afternoon when she awakened again, stretching

in the slanted sunlight, her perfect body moist with the sweat of sleep.

"Oh, I had the most beautiful dream," she sighed. Her eyes opened sleepily and she smiled.

"Please tell me it was true," she whispered.

"Every minute of it," I said, and kissed her.

Queuing Up

⊰ BY CAROLE FEW ⊱

APUNZEL was a bad girl. Of course, she was. Why else'd she be on center stage in The Tower, bent over the heavy leather-covered whipping couch, her limbs firmly captured, her naked ass ready for a whipping? The Tower was a hip, underground sex club in the wildest regions of San Francisco's Mission District. Rapunzel was the fuchsia-haired girl's nickname, because her hair cascaded well past her amazing ass, flowing each time she moved her head. The master up onstage with her was quick to gather her hair in a long ponytail and tie it out of the way. He didn't want to catch her hair instead of her ass with the stroke of the cane. He wanted an unhindered canvas to decorate with the lines of his favored weapon.

The audience immediately booed at him.

"Rapunzel," one of the club kids yelled. "Come on, Rapunzel, sweet Rapunzel, let down your hair!"

The master was having none of the heckling. He lifted his chin to the howling crowd and said, "Quiet now. Unless any of you want a turn after this one." Immediately, several hands went up in the air, other naughty princess types who needed their naked bottoms well punished to the delight of the howling crowd.

"Form a neat queue, then," the British master insisted. "First, I take care of the naughty Rapunzel, and then I will be pleased to deal with anyone else who needs to feel a firm switch on her rebellious arse."

When Rapunzel turned her head, she saw the queue had indeed quickly formed to her left, six creatively dressed sprites, all waiting for their turn to seductively trade in the world of sexual delights for their sins with their flesh. She knew that in minutes her own personal ordeal would be over, and another young woman would have taken her place. But before that happened, she'd be whipped until she screamed, and this is the thought that made her pussy pulse with pleasure. Nothing turned Rapunzel on like a good, thorough punishment session in front of a raucous crowd.

Still, before her master could land the first blow, they heard the call again from the crowd: "Rapunzel, Rapunzel, let down your hair!"

It was a boy yelling, and when Rapunzel searched the faces before her, she saw how handsome he was, how amazingly well built. Why was he so intent on having her hair down? That was the question. The master wasn't interested in playing the boy's game. He wanted the spotlight solely on himself, and he shook his head fiercely at the shouting and said, "You'll be next in line if you don't watch your mouth."

The boy didn't seem to have a problem with that, pushing to the front of the stage and radiating his own attitude right back at the master.

"Move aside, ladies," the master said to the giggling sextet. "This one's over the horse next."

"Bad manners get you to the front of the line," one sprite pouted.

The master didn't hesitate to pounce on her insolence. He hurried to her side, whipped her over his lap, and delivered a stinging hand-paddling on her nearly naked ass before the words were fully out of her mouth. The crowd loved it, going wild at such delightfully impromptu action. The girl was thrown over the master's shoulder and handed off to a muscle-bound bouncer with a shaved head, who stripped her of her translucent dress in less then a second, then easily positioned her on a punishment chair in the corner—first oiling up her anus, then impaling her asshole on the thick dildo sprouting from the center of the chair, and finally placing a sturdy clip on the girl's clit and two more on her nipples. She howled as all of this took place, but it was clear to see that she loved every minute of it.

Rapunzel sighed. She adored scenes like this. But her pussy was screaming now, so ready, and her whole body ached to be taken. And all because that loud, handsome boy had caused a scene. Before she knew what was happening, the master had tied down the lad next to her, so that they were face to face, both over the whipping couch, their bodies exposed. They were so close together that when the master landed his whip, he would undoubtedly be able to catch the two of them.

"Rapunzel," the boy whispered, nuzzling his face against hers. "You're so beautiful, I couldn't let you take this on your own."

She kissed him back as she heard the master announce that he would begin. The first blow wracked her with immediate shudders that vibrated from her to the boy and to her again.

Oh, did she love "bad girl" night at The Tower.

CCCCO

Raver Ali and the Glo-Stick

❧ BY MELODY PERRY ❧

HERE was once a college girl named Alison Dean who was a frustration to her parents and her professors. While everyone knew she was possessed of exceptional cunning, Ali would not apply herself to her studies. Rather, she spent every night she could attending raves in the warehouse district of town, dressing herself up quite scandalously in glow-in-the-dark makeup and psychedelic clothing that swirled when she danced. She would arrive at each happening well before midnight and stay until dawn, pirouetting alone and singing along with the pulsing trance beats.

Ali drew quite a crowd, her dancing having an otherworldly quality that people loved to watch, especially since she tended to favor tighter-than-tight hip-huggers and skintight see-through crop tops to allow her the maximum mobility. Oftentimes both men and women would approach Ali and try to engage her in intimate dancing or invite her upstairs to the chill-out room (also known as the make-out room), where scandalously painted bodies writhed together, luminous in the soft glow of ultraviolet light. But Ali wanted nothing more than to dance all night, and "Fuck off, sleazoid" became one of her most repeated phrases.

Ali's midnight excursions left little time or energy for school, and her grades suffered accordingly.

One night, while she was writhing amid a sea of bodies, she was approached by an older man in a green polo shirt and Dockers.

"My young friend," said the man, leaning annoyingly close to Ali and speaking directly in her ear in order to be heard over the throbbing beat of the techno music. "My name is Mr. Sorce. I'm afraid I've left something in the chill-out room upstairs. Would you be so kind as to retrieve it for me?"

Ali, who was really sick of people trying to pick up on her, continued dancing as if Mr. Sorce had said nothing. She shouted over the music: "Go get it yourself, Grandpa."

"I'm afraid I've been banned from the chill-out room for having a bad vibe. That bouncer Jeanni is a real cunt."

"Hey!" snapped Ali, who had an oddly puritan streak.

"My apologies. If you retrieve my Glo-Stick I shall give you a crisp twenty-dollar bill."

"That's all you want? A Glo-Stick?" Ali scoffed, pirouetting and indicating the scores of scantily clad Peachy Puffs girls who roamed the club with trays of softly glowing tchotchkes. "They're three bucks from the girl with the face paint."

"Yes, but this is a very special Glo-Stick," said Mr. Sorce. "It has sentimental value. You see, it was given to me by my dead lover."

"Dude, bringdown!" said Ali. But she thought about Mr. Sorce's proposal for a moment and decided to accept. Ali had been wanting to freshen up with an Amino Acid

Smoothie from the smart bar, but had given all of her mea-
ger allowance to the Peachy Puffs girls, loading up on lumi-
nescent rubber bracelets and necklaces that now adorned
her body and made such cool swirling trails when she
pirouetted. "All right," she said. "But give me the money up
front."

Mr. Sorce did so, and Ali quickly went up the long stair-
case that led to the chillout room, where couples and
groups retired when they were finished dancing. The
bouncer wore a name badge that said "Jeanni," and gave
Ali a look that would have deeply annoyed the young raver
if Jeanni hadn't had such a smoldering seduction brewing
in her eyes. Instead, Ali, who felt little shyness about
telling large groups of friendship-minded dancers to fuck
off, dropped her eyes and found herself noticing what an
attractive figure Jeanni cut in those skintight snakeskin
pleather pants and knee-high vegan boots.

"Welcome to the makeout room," said Jeanni, her eyes
insistently caressing Ali's body until her nipples became
quite apparent under her skintight crop-top.

Ali opened her mouth to say "Fuck off," but only a low,
rapturous sigh came out. She cleared her throat as Jeanni
looked at her.

"I just need to get something a friend left up here."

"That scumbag Mr. Sorce? He was totally screwing the
vibe in there tearing the place up looking for his stupid
Glo-Stick. I hope he's not really your friend."

"I'll just be a minute," said Ali, and slipped past Jeanni
into the chillout room. Jeanni's eyes followed Ali as she
disappeared into the purple-glowing room with its soft
rhythmic music.

All around were thrift-store couches that had been

covered with silk sheets tie-dyed with fluorescent dye. Couples, threesomes and groups were sprawled in various semirelaxed poses, their hands wandering and their lips locked in explorations of splendid ecstasy. Ali felt her face getting hot; her puritan streak had kept her from visiting the chillout room before.

A quick circuit around the room left Ali feeling somewhat hot and bothered, especially since the music was slow and pulsated with a beat that made her feel quite different than the rapid dance music of the main floor. As she prepared to leave, not having spotted Mr. Sorce's stupid Glo-Stick, she spotted something under one of the couches. It was a Glo-Stick that radiated a color unlike any she'd ever seen. In order to retrieve the Glo-Stick, Ali had to get down on her knees and reach under the squirming legs of a partially disrobed woman whose companion was going down on her. She felt a shiver go through her as she simultaneously touched the Glo-Stick and caught a scent of the woman's musky perfume.

When Ali stood up holding the Glo-Stick, she was immediately confronted with Jeanni, who was standing much closer to Ali than anyone had ever dared to stand on the dance floor without being told to fuck off.

"You found it," said the pleather-clad girl in a husky voice that sent a warm glow from Ali's hand, which clutched the Glo-Stick, down to parts of her body that she rarely thought about (though other people certainly did). "I hope that doesn't mean you'll be leaving?"

With that, Jeanni planted a hard kiss right on Ali's mouth, and her tongue slid insistently past the softly yielding lips. Ali moaned gently as Jeanni eased her back onto a silk-draped sofa and slipped her hands under Ali's tight crop-top, lifting it so she could caress the girl's nipples with her tongue. Soon Ali's pink neon stretch jeans were tangled on the floor and Jeanni was showering her with kisses as Ali clutched the Glo-Stick, moaning.

Suddenly, as Jeanni's mouth descended fiercely between Ali's thighs, Ali felt someone grasping the Glo-Stick and wrenching it out of her hands.

"Thanks for distracting the bouncer," cackled Mr. Sorce, turning to race away with the Glo-Stick. He never made it out the door, however, because a naked girl with glowing plastic bracelets hanging from her body jewelry stuck out her foot and tripped him. With a yelp, Mr. Sorce went sprawling to the floor.

"Dude, you are like totally bringing us down," said the neon-painted girl, and several of her trysting companions nodded in agreement. "Jeanni, can you ask this guy to leave?"

"With pleasure," said Jeanni, planting her boot firmly in Mr. Sorce's ass and kicking him out into the hallway—but not before she'd seized his precious Glo-Stick and wrenched it from his hand.

"And don't make me throw you out a third time," snapped Jeanni as she slammed the door to the chillout room and shot the bolt. With a smile, she returned the Glo-Stick to Ali Dean's hand and took her place between the writhing young raver's spread legs. To thank Jeanni for getting rid of the bad vibe, the other residents of the chillout room, in various states of undress and various states of gender, descended upon Ali Dean and began to caress her all over, an entirely new experience to which Ali Dean, clutching the precious Glo-Stick, gladly succumbed. And though for some time they could hear the pounding and shouting of Mr. Sorce outside the locked door, it wasn't long before another bouncer came and ejected the disruptive patron. After that, the vibe was entirely groovy, and when Jeanni broke out her stash of body paint, things really got going.

And they lived happily ever after, well past dawn.

Stealing Hearts

BY EMILIE PARIS

 HE wasn't a hanging judge so much as she was a "spanking" judge, so when the Knave of Hearts was brought before her, a delicious wave of anticipation shuddered through her. He was a divine specimen indeed: young and handsome, with thick gold curls and the milkiest of milky-white skin. She knew that his crime hardly called for a hearing. Pinching tarts. What a waste of a morning. But he had a record for similar crimes, snitching gingerbread ponies from a neighborhood bakery, disappearing with entire cakes and pies when he had the chance. He must have been riding a sugar high for years, but he'd only been nabbed officially twice before. Now, he was in front of her—and she was called on to deliver a harsh punishment under the kingdom's new "three strikes, you're out" policy.

Still, she had a difficult time keeping a stern expression on her face when she saw how amazingly good-looking he was. Just her type, really. Boyish in his shuffling stature, perhaps, the way he refused to meet her eyes dead on, preferring to duck under that mop of shining hair and glance up at her. Oh, did she love the shy ones. Every once in a while, she found herself strolling the back alleys in her carriage, looking for just this sort of beauty. There was a certain neighborhood behind the kingdom where the young bucks hung out. They'd stand on the corner, hips thrust forward, one hand insolently stroking along a perfect ass. Sometimes they'd be bare-chested. Other times, they'd push their T-shirts aside to show their six-pack abs. She'd have her horseman slow down so that she could choose carefully, even though she knew that if stories of her kinky perversions ever made their way to the royal press, her career would be over. Sometimes cravings were impossible to deny.

That's why she went easy on this knave. She knew all about cravings.

Even with the three-strikes law in place, she was able to find a loophole, one that released the Knave of Hearts into her own personal care. As soon as the tedious paperwork was complete, she led the boy out to the carriage. He hadn't spoken a word to her yet, seemed stunned to find himself in the late-afternoon light, rather than back in a cold stone cell, wearing iron manacles that allowed no way to gain comfort. It was as if he thought that, by speaking, the whole scene might dissolve into a fairy tale fantasy—that he might awake to find himself chained to the rock wall beneath the courtroom.

Within the safety of the carriage, she nodded to him. "Now," she said, "you can say anything you want. It's only you and me. Nobody else can hear us. Nobody else will know."

The carriage swung gently into motion and then gradually picked up speed.

"Why?" he asked.

That was simple enough. And she had an answer.

"I didn't think the system could properly punish you—"

"No?"

"No," she shook her head, and with the movement, her long black hair spilled free from the tight confines of her severe bun. "I think I'm much better able to handle the job at my château."

As she said the words, she saw him blush, and the coloring to his pale skin made her heart beat extra quickly. Oh, what fun she would have trying to break this boy. She'd reward him for good behavior with a plate of heart-shaped tarts, but only after he took the medicine she longed to dole out. Ten lashes, perhaps? They could start small, start simply.

Suddenly she felt his hand on her knee, his fingers probing beneath the red-embroidered hem of her velvet gown. She should push his hand away, she knew that, establish right from the start who was boss. But the boy was soon on the floor of the carriage, spreading her thighs for her, using his hands to push her legs open wide. And then he had his mouth pressed to her, under her dress but on top of her various layers of undergarments, so that she could feel the heat of his breath through the cloth barriers. She groaned and grabbed hold of him, pushing him even more firmly against her.

The boy knew how to please. His tongue and his fingers worked her at a quickening pace, until she had to stand, to kick off her pantaloons and petticoats, to lift her dress up high so that when she sat again he had clean, unhindered access to her sex. Immediately he went back to work on her, looping his tongue in gently growing circles, caressing her clit with his lips until she felt herself coming. Thoughts

of how they might play later filled her mind. She easily envisioned the handsome boy over her lap, her bare hand
punishing his naked haunches.

The first time he'd been caught, the king had done this
himself: beating the knave full sore. And yet, the discipline
hadn't had the desired effect. He hadn't lost his taste for
thievery. She could make him mind, she knew. She could
change him, until the only thing he craved was punishment
at her own hand. How he'd live to serve her. How he'd
learn to love every painful moment—

The boy spoke as this image blossomed within her.

"Three strikes," he said. "I knew it was the only way to
meet you."

Her eyes grew wide. "You did it on purpose, then?"

His cheeks turned a darker shade of sunset pink, and he
nodded, his mouth glistening wet with the sweet honeyed
juices of her sex. "I've heard about you," he said. "Underground whispers about the Judge of Hearts. I knew that
you had what I need—"

"And that's why—" she started.

"Why I pinched the tarts. But I promise," he said, "I
mean, I vow—"

"To steal no more?" she finished for him.

Bending low to kiss her feet, he answered the question
for her.

ccccoo

The Trials of Lady Vicarious

⇥ BY SAGE VIVANT ⇤

I am Lady Vicarious and this is the tale of my corruption.

I have served milady, the Princess Oralia, since the dawn of my own womanhood. We are separated by only a handful of years. My mother, Lady Tedium, had served before me, and I observed her ministrations closely so as not to displease the beautiful princess.

Our association began with a closeness far beyond that of many dear friends. When the princess was irritable, I would massage her massive breasts until she heaved such a sigh of relief that she immediately required sleep. To my surprise, she would sometimes sneak up behind me while I performed some mundane household task and caress my own breasts until my knees wobbled and I could work no longer. I ask you—how many princesses do you know who fondle the bosoms of their servants? She was a pearl amid a sea of common pebbles.

I did her bidding without complaint or question. So, when she asked me to lure Lothar the Viscous to her palace in Orgiastica, I did not balk. Instead, I listened closely to her instruction.

"Samspaden sends word that Lothar the Viscous and his tribe have camped on the outskirts of the kingdom," she said with great seriousness as she lay topless on her plushly upholstered bed. Filmy chiffon veils covered her long, luscious legs.

"Does milady fear an invasion?" I queried.

"Perhaps," she caught my eye, and her brilliant blue irises flashed like ice shards. I knew she was thinking very hard.

"Will we send troops to crush them?"

"No, not just yet. I have heard much about this barbaric tribe, none of it good. Lothar in particular is known for his incessant come-spewing. His foes say that his member is so large and constantly erect that he wields it like an iron club, smiting his enemies with blows so wet and sloppy that death by drowning is not uncommon." Princess Oralia reached between her thighs and fingered herself absently. It was an adorable habit she'd had since puberty. Sometimes I would do it for her if she needed her hands free for other activities.

I was aghast at this Lothar and his unorthodox combat methods. And so, as the princess continued, my awe did not abate.

"I do not wish to have my troops blinded or battered by Lothar the Viscous. Rather than fight him, I believe we must capture him and lock him up where he can be a threat to no one but himself. I wonder if he will spew without provocation?" Her hand moved faster and I heard her juices squish about her fingers. Her eyes took on a distant look.

"We shall surprise him with courtesy," Princess Oralia purred, grinning broadly at me. "I need you to travel to his camp and invite him to Orgiastica on my behalf. Tell him I wish to entertain him and whatever entourage he requires. Emphasize that you come in peace." She brought her fingers to her mouth now, licking them with satisfied decisiveness.

I confess to some trepidation. I had never seen a male member, let alone one that oozed and smote unsuspecting persons. Never would I reveal my fear to milady, however.

"Shall I alert any of milady's subjects of this imminent journey?" I inquired, secretly and desperately hoping to learn that a battalion would accompany me.

"Certainly not," Princess Oralia replied. "You are to appear by yourself, without the implied support that my troops would convey. Lothar must see that my offer is genuine. You will travel alone. Go now and return him to me by nightfall next."

I had never been so frightened in all my young life. The princess helped me dress, insisting that the fabric around my nipples be removed so that they would point plaintively at Lothar when I extended the invitation. I set out on my journey, trembling inwardly, my hard pink nipples leading the way.

Fortunately, the kingdom is small enough to be traversed in less than a day, and so I arrived at the barbarian encampment just before sunset.

Several barbarians shouted and applauded at my entrance, all of them replacing the spears in their hands with firm, throbbing penises. I grasped the reins of my horse more tightly so I wouldn't slide off the animal. I said nothing as I watched hordes of them beat off in oddly syncopated rhythms. I rode toward the largest tent, assuming Lothar would be ensconced there.

As I approached, a mighty roar resounded through the wood, and I instinctively knew I'd found the infamous Lothar. A thin stream of thick, viscous fluid flowed by me as confirmation. My horse stepped around it, as if out of respect.

And yet, I was not prepared for the immense specter of a man I encountered. With his guard tied to a tree some yards away, the massive barbarian gripped his pulsating member with both hands, flinging it wildly about and milking an endless rope of come from its bulbous head. The guard dripped with the gooey consequences of Lothar's actions.

In my compromised travel attire, I had not a shield to hold before me to protect myself from Lothar the Viscous. He sprayed me quite soundly even before he realized I was there. Upon noting my existence, he paused to drool at my exposed nipples. By now, the entire camp had collected around us, eager for a show.

"Big, buxom beauty!" He bellowed, aiming his member at me. "Dismount and be skewered!"

I sat frozen, unable to fathom what orifice of mine could possibly accommodate this enormous manpiece. As I considered my prospects, my saddle absorbed the abundant moisture soaking through my skirt. I tried to remember my mission.

"Forgive the intrusion, kind sir. My name is Lady Vicarious and I come in peace. As you can see, I travel alone and mean no harm. Am I addressing the great Lothar the Viscous?"

He spewed a goblet's worth of his seed at me and winked. I decided against wiping it from my face and hair.

"I am he! What do you want with me if not to enjoy my viscosity?"

"I come with an invitation from Princess Oralia, ruler of Orgiastica. She wishes to entertain you and whatever entourage you desire at her castle tomorrow evening. I am to be your escort."

"Not before I and my men suck those ample teats of yours, Lady Vicarious!"

I cannot say how many barbarians descended upon me. I was removed from my horse, and my bodice was torn open. My breasts popped out at the crowd like ripe, round fruit. Though each of my breasts is the size of a human head, so many tongues covered them that my mounds disappeared from my view. I had not expected such intense pleasure from this experience, but in minutes I heard myself shouting such indecencies as "Suck me!" and "Impale me *now!*"

It is my belief that my corruption began at this moment.

They tore the remainder of my clothes from my body before they impaled me on the helpless guard. Oh, the divine cleaving of my swollen maidenhead! I nearly swooned as they raised and lowered me on his manhood. So many times did they slide the fleshy rod into me that I lost consciousness.

When I awoke, I, too, was tied to the tree. The guard, still tied, snored loudly. His manhood, still hard, had been stuffed inside me, and my insides still gripped it tightly. Lothar stood nearby, obviously waiting for me to become conscious again. He cocked his head at me.

"Does Princess Oralia boast breasts like your own?"

"Of course. Such breasts are a requisite of citizenship in Orgiastica."

"Untie the wench!" He commanded his troops. "We're going to pay a visit to the princess!"

They rode behind me in relative silence. Lothar directed his viscous emissions at the scenery, rather than at me, for which I was grateful. My clothes, ripped and destroyed beyond recognition, did little to shelter me from the cool forest air.

Lothar asked only one other barbarian to join him—his guard. I interpreted this act as a demonstration of trust and good faith on his part. I was proud of my princess for her sophisticated and successful strategy. I did wonder, though, how she planned to restrain and capture the moist and mighty Lothar.

Princess Oralia is renowned for her beauty so it was no surprise when Lothar erupted in particularly vehement spurts upon meeting her. She exuded terror and shielded her face from his sticky onslaught.

"Please sir! I have invited you here in peace. Be mindful that it is only I and my lady-in-waiting, two helpless women unable to defend ourselves against your brute strength and force. I beg of you to restrain your come-spewing!"

I had never seen the princess plead. She must have been truly frightened by the immense barbarian.

He leered at the princess and walked toward her. The guard swiftly grasped the fabric at her luscious cleavage and yanked downward, ripping her lovely gown open. Though she blushed, her eyes flashed in what I could only imagine was challenge. I knew the princess did not like to lose, yet she did not scream or struggle.

"I am appalled by your behavior, sir! If it continues, I shall have to ask you to leave."

He drew closer, sliding his slippery anatomical club between her heaving breasts and squeezing them together. His fluid coated her chest in minutes as he held her gaze.

"Nice to meet you, Princess Oralia," he drawled as globs of come fell from her big globes to the floor. "So, where's this entertainment your lady-in-waiting promised?"

The princess turned her head to speak, for the tip of the barbarian's member threatened to impair her speech.

"I thought we would begin with a fine feast of mutton and mead," she began with uncharacteristic shyness.

He squirted a stripe across her face. "Ha! The only feast I want is you eating my mighty cock!" he thundered.

Retreating to a nearby chair, he pulled her by her big, erect nipples. The guard reached under her skirts and appeared to hold her ass in his palms. The princess did not protest. Instantly, she sat at his feet and buried her pretty face in his bulging, sticky crotch. She licked him noisily, lapping at his semen as if it were indeed a tasty meal.

"Guard! Make Lady Vicarious eat you, too!" Lothar commanded.

And so I soon found myself sucking off the man who'd robbed me of my virginity the night before. I did not even know his name.

I glanced over at milady for guidance, for it was clear that she was of no small experience in the art of cocksucking. Lothar's wet enthusiasm matted her hair and coated her face and neck, yet she was not deterred. She ate him with gusto, which only increased his gooey flow. I tried my best to emulate her and was secretly grateful that the guard did not ejaculate as profusely as his leader.

"Stand, Princess!"

She obeyed.

"Bend over and show me the flower buried between your cheeks!"

"No! Oh, no, sir! You do wrong me beyond measure! I am pure and chaste and unaccustomed to displaying myself so wantonly."

Nevertheless, she turned and showed him that which he requested. The guard instructed me likewise.

As Lothar's seething manhood explored the sopping recesses of the princess, I felt the shame of wetness between my legs. The guard's manliness spread that wetness all around my engorged private places.

Lothar rammed the princess with a mighty thrust that nearly upset her balance. She bit her lip as her eyes rolled upward.

"No, Lothar! Stop! I beg you!" She gasped, pushing her royal arse toward him. She reached between her legs to stroke her slick folds. When I followed her lead, I discovered the wonderful wisdom of such a move. Between the guard's forceful slams and my busy fingers at my swollen bud, some kind of explosion took place within me. The room spun, I heard myself shouting, and the walls of my inner canal clutched at the guard's meaty rod until I collapsed, barely aware of my surroundings.

The guard let go of himself and sprayed me in erratic outbursts that, in my dreamlike state, felt like caresses.

"No, no! You mustn't!" advised Princess Oralia as Lothar slowly inserted himself up her other, tighter channel. When he began to pound her, she dropped to her knees.

"Stop this instant!" she wailed, now moving her hand to his enormous sac. He slid off the chair and sat on his ankles. He lifted the princess to his lap and bounced her there as he grabbed her bobbing breasts.

The princess squealed and in my stupor I wondered if she felt pain or pleasure. She threw her arms over her head and wrapped them around his neck. Still, he stuffed himself into her with great force.

And then it happened.

A shower of viscous fluid rained down on all of us. I could not see through it. The force of it created great splattering sounds everywhere. The guard held my face down so I could continue to breathe. The storm lasted several minutes. When at last it stopped, I found myself in a veritable pool. Lothar sat slumped against the wall. His manhood, still erect and enormous, oozed nothing. His eyes were closed.

Princess Oralia crawled through the muck to grab my arm, dragging me across the room to the door. When at last we reached it, she stood to pull the lever near the threshold. I watched as the two men, spent and vulnerable, dropped through the massive trap doors and disappeared into the dungeon below.

As the days passed and the princess spent more and more time in the dungeon, I asked why we did not punish the barbarians. Or starve them to death.

"It is up to us to sap them of their strength," the princess explained.

"We must milk the mighty Lothar of all power and end the loathsome come-spewing once and for all. It is the only way we can keep the kingdom safe."

I must confess, dear reader, that I doubted the veracity of milady's intentions. Having experienced the sublime pleasure of being deflowered, I knew any woman would seek repeat performances.

Though I had been corrupted, never would I be guilty of insurgence or insubordination. And so I assisted milady by milking the guard of his strength, sometimes several times a day.

I believe we have much work ahead of us.

Undressed

⧈ BY JESSE NELSON ⧈

 stared at myself in the dressing-room mirror, listening to the clucks of approval from the obsequious clerk standing behind me. In a haughty tone, he claimed the suit fit me "to perfection," but when I looked, all I saw was a pin-striped gray wool automaton. Didn't seem right to me, even though the outfit was as expensive as all hell. Money can't buy style. I learned that early on. Most people haven't got a handle on that one yet.

"You don't like the cut, sir?" the clerk asked, concern furrowing his handsome brow. He was obviously envisioning his swiftly vanishing commission.

I shook my head. I couldn't easily explain what was wrong. All I knew was that the outfit was not in the least bit festive. Not at all unique. But what did I expect, after all? I'd come to a place where people paid to look like everyone else. The uniform was chic enough; that didn't make a difference in this case. I stripped down and put my own clothes back on—Levi's, T-shirt, and sweater. Now, I looked like me again, but this wasn't the right attire, either.

Finally, I decided I'd have to bring Glenda into the deliberations. My girlfriend has an uncanny style sense, and this was *her* friend's party, after all. I'd been trying to prove to myself—and to her—that I had enough know-how to put together an outfit. But I proved wrong.

Glenda was thrilled to be asked. "Don't worry, Tommy," she told me. "I have the perfect place to take you."

I should have been wary. And I should have known exactly where she'd take me. One of her all-time favorite stores, down the street from her apartment on Melrose, an upscale consignment store overflowing with finery from days gone by. Or, more honestly, from the '70s. When I saw the wide ties and the polka-dotted shirts, the fake fur and the plaid—oh, Jesus, the plaid—I almost turned around. Glenda had a firm grip on me, and she pushed me forward.

"Not my style," I told her.

"You promised to trust me," she responded.

Generally, I'm about suits or Levi's. I work as a lawyer in a conservative practice. Can't get away with scuffed shoes at the office, even in California. Glenda's in the movies, a costume designer on the biggest-budget endeavors. She adds class to any scene, adds considerable style points even to me, just by being on my arm. Now I was putting myself in her knowledgeable hands—why did that freak me out so much?

While I teetered on the verge of losing my cool, Glenda busied herself gathering armloads of clothes. Then, after shooting me an "I'm ready" look, we went into the dressing room together. I hated everything she'd chosen. Wasn't me. Wasn't my scene. But I forced a patient expression onto my face and tried each outfit she presented me with. Couldn't she see how uncomfortable I was in the baggy pants and suspenders? The skinny tie and rockabilly shirt? The dyed black denims with stovepipe legs? Didn't she know that my general look is not only one of convenience but one of comfort. I like to blend in. That's precisely what my uniform does for me. Turns me into part of the crowd.

Of course, she understood. That's why she was having so much fun. With her orange and purple numbers, the swirls and patterns, she was in a psychedelic dream come true. "Relax, Tommy," she hissed at me. "You're not having a good time at all, only because you've got that stick up your ass."

"This ass?" I said, posing for her in my BVDs. "That's what you think the trouble is?"

She stifled a laugh. "I know *that's* not the trouble." She took a moment to admire my rear view. "But you have to start letting go a little. This is a costume party, after all. You can't wear a suit and be a lawyer."

"But that's who I am."

"Exactly. The costume part of the party means dressing up as something you're not." She said this with a bit of exasperation, as if she couldn't understand why I wouldn't do things her way. Part of the reason we're such a good couple is that we're so different—but every once in a while our headstrong ways meet in the middle and we find we can neither go forward nor back.

Which is when she got the idea. I could see it happening, her eyes widening, her mouth parting. "Why didn't I think of that earlier?" she cooed to herself, pushing the pile of clothing aside.

"What do you mean?"

"Trust me," she said again, leading me from the store and back up the hill to her place. "Just trust me."

In her apartment, she let me watch her dress herself. She was going as Eve, with well-placed fig leaves strategically hiding her most lovely assets. Then she blindfolded me and told me to stand up in front of her. This wasn't the first time we'd played sensory deprivation games, but it was the first time we did so outside of a strictly sexual situation. Maybe that's why I got hard so quickly. I felt slippery garments moving over my body, felt her angling and arranging items to suit her. I wished I could see, but Glenda said no, and when she says no, I listen. That's another reason why we're such a good team. At home, behind closed doors, she's the one in charge. It's always been that way with us, and I revel in giving up my power to her, and all the insane complications that power brings with it.

She took me in her car, still wearing the blindfold, and then drove us in near-silence for twenty minutes. The only sounds were the traffic around us and Glenda's occasional murmurings to herself, snippets of song lyrics that she had a habit of singing—out of nowhere—Bono. Dylan. The Stones.

Finally, she parked and ushered me still blindfolded into the party. It was at one of those mansions, way up in the hills, and I could tell from the noise level, the mixtures of expensive perfume and scent of alcohol in the air, that the place was crushed with people. I heard them stop when we entered.

There she goes again, I thought. *My Glen, cutting a scene.*

I felt her remove my overcoat, and then I felt her fingers working rapidly, and then gusts of warm air against me, and I thought I understood.

But no—she wouldn't have done that, would she?

Oohs and aahs sounded immediately around us, and Glenda took my hand and moved me into the midst of the partiers. Again, I thought that thought. The unthinkable thought. I could feel fabric. I wasn't naked. Was I?

"So lovely, Glenny," someone cooed to her.

"You've done it again."

"A masterpiece."

I grabbed onto the blindfold, but Glenda hissed at me. "Stop, or I won't reward you. Tonight will be a lonely, pleasureless night if you disobey me." So I allowed her to take me, still blinded, through her entire scene, until she felt the location was right. Only then did she tell me I could remove the scarf. When she did, I found that we were in the master bathroom, in a room of mirrors, wall upon wall of mirrors. And I found that yes, I was naked, and no, I was not. She'd put me in a gauzy layer of entirely sheer fabric. A suit of nothing.

A naked suit.

The story came together in my head suddenly: *The Emperor's New Clothes,* with each fawning attendee oohing and aahing over something that wasn't there at all. And yet in this story, the lack of clothing wasn't a cruel trick, or an evil surprise, but the best gift my girlfriend could ever have given me. Because suddenly the door opened and the partyers hurried in, as many as could fit in the room, and there were hands on me, and mouths on me, open and kissing me, fingers probing, skin on skin.

I felt the rustling rush of a fresh mouth on my cock, and I looked to see Glenda urging a lovely young starlet to drink me down. She was blonde and winsome with a peony-painted mouth that she parted wide in order to grant me access. As I felt the wet heat of her mouth close around my rod, I turned my head to see the prettiest brunette begin working her pussy in front of me, hitched up on the marble counter, legs spread, letting me watch as she teased herself on toward a magnificent orgasm. Another couple began to fuck right next to me, their bodies so close, their emotions so raw. I could feel their breaths, sense their shudders and shivers of each forward thrust.

My eyes were in constant motion, trying to drink in every erotic image that whirred around me. The spike-haired boy going down on his girlfriend in the marble shower. The handsome older man instructing a svelte redhead in the interesting uses of the bidet. When Glenda suddenly pushed the startled ingenue out of the way, and she took her rightful position on the floor, sucking me hard, all the way down to the root so that her lips pressed against my skin. I liked that her lipstick was smeared, even though I hadn't seen her kissing anyone. I liked that she didn't have a problem swapping spit with the vixen who'd been locked to my cock only moments before.

I liked it all.

She deep-throated me like a pro, and I had to put my hands out for a moment, feeling dizzy with the pleasure, finding it an effort simply to stay standing, to remain in an upright and locked position. Immediately, several partyers came to my aid, moving closer, supporting me with their own bodies, keeping me steady so that I could enjoy every second of Glenda blowing me in front of all those people. All those curious, watching, ravenous people.

And I got. Suddenly, I got it.

Stripped down, and *un*dressed, without the comfort and safety of my standard uniform, I felt more free than I ever have before.

ⓒⓒⓒⓒⓒ

A Very Golden Goosing

‚⊰ BY ANDRE FARMER ⊱∘

 OLDIE Gosling had lived all her life in the luxury apartment building on the Upper East Side. She and her parents both loved the place. She remembered being very young and frightened by the elevator operators; it seemed so strange to have this uniformed gentleman, polite and refined to a fault, privy to all the private conversations one might choose to have in the elevator. This was particularly true because Goldie and her parents lived on the fifty-seventh floor, so they invariably had quite a ride ahead of them when they entered the building. Still, the operators were always quite respectful.

That is, until Jimmy.

Goldie was eighteen and Jimmy not much older when he came to work at the building. From the moment Goldie set eyes on him, she was captured. He was gorgeous, with his thick black hair cut in a rakish manner, his full pink lips looking astonishingly kissable. Goldie had never been kissed, having attended an exclusive Manhattan girls' school and being forbidden by her parents to date. They had agreed to lift that restriction when she started Columbia in the fall, provided she lived at home.

But she wanted to kiss Jimmy very much. There was something about the pearly pale cast of his skin, the well-muscled cut of his body, the faint scar across his jawline, the suspicious narrowing of the eyes, the small sarcastic smile that always seemed to be twisting his lips in a way that, Goldie suspected, was so subtle that no one but her noticed. All she had to do was *think* about getting on an elevator and she started to get excited. Jimmy's Brooklyn accent echoed in her ears whenever she dreamed of him—streetwise and confident.

But she played it cool, not wanting to seem easy. After all, she had to wait another two months before she'd even be allowed to date. And certainly her parents wouldn't sit still if she decided to date an elevator operator, would they?

Nonetheless, Goldie found her midnight visions filled with Jimmy, imagining him kissing her, touching her, making love to her. She wondered what other scars he bore on that muscled body underneath that conservative red uniform. She had her first orgasm thinking of Jimmy, sprawled in the covers under her bed biting her finger very hard so as not to issue the passionate moans that were surging up inside her body. Her finger had teeth marks for three days.

Each time she entered the elevator Goldie could smell him, his rough scent of blended male musk, machine oil, and Brylcreem. Her pussy would clench firmly remembering the frequent fantasies of Jimmy atop her, moaning as he lost that cool exterior, trading it for a torrent of lust for her.

But Jimmy remained distant, aloof, despite the way his

eyes roved over Goldie whenever she stepped into the elevator. He was always coolly polite. He never offered her more than a "Good morning, Miss Gosling" or a "Good evening, Miss Gosling." He never even asked her how she was doing.

The night it happened, she had been at the library very late, studying for her final exam in her summer school class on the philosophy of quantum physics at the NYU Extension Program. She was quite sure to get an A, but there's nothing wrong with getting an A+, is there? The chauffeur dropped her off in front of the building and watched to make sure the doorman was on duty before parking the car.

Sleepy and somewhat giddy with exhaustion, Goldie found herself the only person on the elevator. Against her better judgment, she entered.

"Good morning, Miss Gosling," said Jimmy, his eyes flickering up and down Goldie's body. She felt somewhat ashamed that she'd worn a brief summer dress that left her quite exposed, but it got so *hot* in that library.

Goldie said, "Oh, is it after midnight?"

"Just barely, Miss Gosling," said Jimmy, his eyes never leaving her body, lingering over the way her full breasts filled out the dress.

"Then good morning, Jimmy. Busy night?"

"It is now," he said.

Puzzling at that last comment, Goldie turned around and faced the door. The elevator hummed silently to life, and without warning, Goldie felt a sudden pinch on her pussy. She gasped, leaping forward. She looked at Jimmy with horror. He looked like the cat who ate the canary.

"Something wrong, Miss Gosling?"

Goldie felt a tiny shiver go through her lower regions, her pussy swelling and moistening with the touch of Jimmy's hand. He *had* touched her, hadn't he? Or perhaps she had just imagined it.

"Nothing's wrong," she said, turning back around. "Nothing at all."

Another pinch, and this time Goldie didn't turn around. Then Jimmy's hand was on her more firmly, and she was pushing back onto him as he stroked her pussy, finding it wet. Goldie shut her eyes very tight as the long journey up to the fifty-seventh floor whirred on in moaning shroud. "Don't turn around," Jimmy said, just to make sure, and Goldie seized the grab rails as her orgasm exploded through her.

Jimmy's hand withdrew, and Goldie stood on unsteady legs as the doors slid open.

"Fifty-seventh floor," said Jimmy. "Good night, Miss Gosling."

"Good . . . good night, Jimmy," she said, her voice hoarse.

Goldie didn't get a wink of sleep that night. She thrashed in her bed, moaning as she remembered Jimmy touching her—and pictured him doing more. Kissing her. Undressing her. Fucking her for the first time up against that elevator wall on the long journey to the fifty-seventh floor.

For the rest of the summer, Goldie started making a habit of studying late—very late. Jimmy was an expert; he could always make her come before the fifty-seventh floor, provided she followed his instructions and didn't turn around. Within a few weeks she was climaxing on thirty-four, then twenty-four. Jimmy had her getting off three times on some nights before they reached fifty-seven—all without touching her anywhere except her pussy.

Goldie's pussy remained in a perpetual ache, as she was rubbing herself violently to orgasm every night after her trip with Jimmy. She dreamed of him always. She believed she was in love.

The day before classes began at Columbia, the ever-fastidious Goldie was at the library well past midnight studying her schoolbooks to make sure she would be ahead of the game on the very first day. She returned from the library with Jimmy on her mind. She had been thinking of him all evening as she studied, and the mere sight of him made her melt.

"Good morning, Miss Gosling. Particularly late tonight, aren't you?"

"Yes, Jimmy," she said. "Good morning."

Goldie trembled as she turned around.

The elevator whirred to life and Goldie took the grab rails, supporting herself as Jimmy's fingers slipped under her skirt, under her panties, and began stroking her. Suddenly, she couldn't take it anymore.

She hit the emergency stop button and launched herself at Jimmy, wrapping her arms and legs around him as she pressed her lips to his.

"The surveillance camera—" he said weakly, but then his protests were lost in moans as Goldie dropped to her knees and clawed his red uniform pants open. His cock in her mouth tasted even sweeter than she'd dreamed of, all the nights she pictured herself doing exactly this. She sucked him hungrily as Jimmy ran his magic fingers through her hair.

But she wanted more. Goldie took her mouth off Jimmy's cock, looked up into his beautiful eyes and whispered, "Fuck me."

Jimmy lifted Goldie onto her feet and pushed her against the wall of the elevator, propping her ass on the railing as he tugged her underwear to one side and entered her. Goldie felt only the slightest twinge of discomfort as Jimmy's hard cock opened her pussy for the very first time—and then it was nothing but ecstasy, as she came on Jimmy's cock, his hands roving all over her body and tearing her dress until it was nothing but shreds. She came slumped against him, moaning as he emptied himself inside her.

Goldie was very lucky that her parents were already asleep. She slipped inside and tucked her dress down the garbage chute—there wasn't much left of it, anyway. She slept fitfully for the rest of the night, awakening periodically to touch herself and thunder eagerly and repeatedly into the throes of orgasm as she dreamed of her next elevator encounter with Jimmy.

But when Goldie entered the elevator, wearing a smart businesslike outfit of navy blue for her first day at Columbia, some elderly man she'd never seen was operating the elevator.

"What happened to Jimmy?" she asked.

"Oh, I'm afraid he's been fired," said the new elevator operator. He chuckled and nudged her in the ribs. "I heard he had a bit of a toss with one of the tenants right here in this very elevator. Shocking, eh? He was fired on the spot."

Goldie wept all the way uptown on the subway. She hid her face and bawled. Her skin tingled all over remembering the touches Jimmy had given her, and her pussy clenched remembering how he'd entered her for the first time, making her come as he crushed her against the elevator wall.

Never again. She had made a slut of herself and she would never see Jimmy again.

Her eyes were bloodshot and her cheeks were pink as she walked, fifteen minutes early, into her class on existential despair and the twenty-first-century mind. She sat miserably in the back row—she had never sat in the back row in her whole life, always choosing the front so she could ask pertinent questions and impress her teachers. Now, though, poor Goldie just wanted to disappear.

Her face was buried in a copy of *Being and Nothingness* that was rapidly edging toward the Nothingness side as Goldie's tears soaked its pages.

"Yo, you're gonna ruin that book, lady."

Goldie looked up, staring wide-eyed at the familiar sound of Jimmy's Brooklyn accent. Jimmy wore a tight white T-shirt and blue jeans folded up over his engineer boots. He had a pack of Lucky Strikes wrapped up in the sleeve, their colorful logo just visible through the white cotton. He had a motorcycle helmet crooked under one arm and a backpack over the other shoulder. There was a copy of Plato tucked alongside the helmet.

Tears streamed down Goldie's face.

"I . . . I got you fired," she said.

Jimmy shrugged. "Ah, I didn't need that job anyway. I just had to keep it for the summer in order to hang on to my scholarship. Now that the term's started, I'll do okay. I mean, hey, you wanna get out of Brooklyn and be a philosophy professor, you gotta play by the rules. I wouldn't have kept that job anyway. Listen, you wanna get a cappuccino after class?"

The professor took the podium and said pretentiously: "Desire. What is the place for desire, desire that ascends to the stars from the lowest depths of human misery?"

Goldie threw her arms around Jimmy and kissed him.

Wicked Sisters

BY MILA WHITELY

HE stepsisters are always evil. Think about it. In every fairy tale you'll ever read, the stepsisters are evil and ugly, deformed either in their looks or in their personalities, or both. But that's not fair. Some of them are simply misunderstood. Or, some of *us*, I should say. And I'm getting a little bit tired of the bad rap, to tell you the truth. Who wouldn't be miffed by always being described as bitchy? Or ignorant? Or downright dangerous? We've been relentlessly portrayed as dowdy dressers. Bad singers. Whiners who are unusually cruel and self-centered.

And let me tell you something else. The princesses aren't always as good as they seem. Everyone has a bad day every once in a while, you know? Even beauties like Cinderella. Stop in during *her* time of the month, and you'll get a completely different view, if you know what I mean. Especially, now that she got married. Just look at her new lot in life. There's a lot more responsibility when you're royalty than when you're simply an average Jane.

Speaking of names, I'd like to turn your attention back to me. Me and my sister. What chance did we even have with names like Drusilda and Esmerelda? No guy wants to wrangle with a mouthful of a name like that. No one coos it in your ear during heavy petting sessions. "Oh, Drusilda—" Just doesn't work. We were burned from the start. Which is why, when I left home shortly after Cindy's wedding, I changed my name immediately to Drue. Short and sweet. To suit my new personality, I ditched the gray draping clothing, hit the gym, and did about a year with a heavy-duty therapist who convinced me that by hanging on to family baggage, I was holding myself back.

Moving across the country helped. Getting a job at a tattoo/piercing parlor was the next step in my transformation. I immediately locked into the underground hip world of the artists I was working with. I chopped off my hair and had it dyed rich cobalt blue, got a few piercings myself, and felt worlds better. By the time Cindy showed up with her Prince on an anniversary trip to Hollywood, she didn't even recognize me. (We'd lost touch over the years, as might be expected with extraneous family members, and even when her annual pious Christmas letter did find its way to me, I rarely bothered to read it. If I worked to keep track of all my steprelatives, I'd never get anything done.)

The couple arrived late in the afternoon on a Saturday with a request that had Cindy written all over it. They wanted double tattoos, she said, matching half-heart shapes that when placed together would become whole. Placed together. What a crock! They'd have to sprawl hip to hip to make the tattoos match, and who ever does that in the real world?

Although I was sitting at the counter, blowing smoke rings toward the ceiling fan, Cindy ignored me in favor of my coworker, Paul. She's always been like that, had a thing for male authority figures. (We won't get into why *she* needs therapy at this point. That's another story entirely.) I listened for several minutes to her describing in her know-it-all-way exactly what she wanted to Paul.

"Let me do this," I said, standing up.

Paul gave me a little shrug and went back to his coffee and crossword puzzle. I led Cindy into one room and her Prince into the other. Cindy didn't even glance at me. She was so into herself, she spent the whole time looking in the mirror as I did her heart. But I looked her over, soaking in the fact that she was quite a bit blonder and a few pounds heavier than she'd been when dolled up in that lace concoction of a wedding gown. I wondered if she'd ever really look up at me and place my face, but she was far too enthralled with her own reflection.

"Hon," she called out to her man when I'd finished, "I'm going to shop the strip while you get yours."

I liked the sound of that. While he got his. What did that mean precisely? I thought about the fact that *I'd* actually seen him first, back at the ball all those years ago, and I remembered an interested look he'd shot me before Cindy appeared in her magic outfit and that stupid pumpkin-into-crystal carriage.

"I know you," he said as I pushed through the heavy jet beaded curtains.

"Yeah."

"Dru—" he started.

"That's it. Just Drue."

"Can't believe Cindy didn't realize."

"Not everyone does."

"But you're *kin*—"

"Sure, but I went through a big transformation."

"Yeah," he nodded. "You look fucking amazing."

That felt good to hear. Not that I have anything invested in how others see me, but I did feel fine being admired by her man. So now it was time for me and the Prince, and I spent a little longer with him, which is to say that I used my mouth on his rod just to see if I could. I'll say this—he didn't complain. He didn't make a move, as if scared that I might stop if he said a word, or changed his position in even the most minute manner.

With my lips pursed, I suckled him expertly. I wanted that pole of his to be spit-slicked and shiny for me by the time I was ready to ride him. In between long, luscious licks, I lingered on his balls, kissing sweetly, lapping like a kitten. Then back I went to his cock, using suction now, feeling him grow in my mouth.

As soon as I had him all wet, I kicked out of my boots and faded black jeans and climbed on board. I didn't have panties on—rarely wear them—so nothing got in our way as I worked my body up and down. It felt good. Really good. I get the most out of any fuck session. That's the way I am. Selfish? Sure, when it comes to sex I think there should be two winners—but I always plan to reach the finish line first. For some reason, this time I was almost coming from the very start. Maybe it was the illicitness of the act. Doing it not only with a married man, but a man who was wedded to my stepsister. Maybe it was because we were at work, and I'd fantasized for quite a while about getting it on with one of my clients. Whatever the reason, I was hot and ready myself. I swiveled my hips and pushed up and then back down on him, filling myself with his huge, thick cock. While we fucked, I gazed at his handsome face. The years had been kinder to him than to Cindy. His glorious dark hair was graying at the temple, but his jaw was just as strong and his eyes as piercing blue.

He couldn't believe his luck. Let me tell you, it was obvious he hadn't gotten any serious fucking in months. From the way he responded, it might even have been years. "It was all my dad—" he started to say, but I shook my head. I didn't want to hear excuses now. "And that stupid shoe," he continued, and I smiled, remembering that whole scene. Foot fetishists must have had a field day reading in the paper about each girl in town taking her turn at trying on the slipper.

"You didn't even try."

"I knew it wouldn't fit me."

"Right," he said, "wasn't your style."

I thought about the most recent Christmas letter that I'd actually read. The one that said they were living in a world of total refined bliss. Perhaps, refined bliss didn't allow for oral sex, or midday sex, or (maybe) *any* sex.

"Missed you, Drue," he said, and I shrugged. Too much time gone by to think about other possible endings to fairy tales.

Now, he used his hands on my waist to anchor me, and he pushed me up and back, helping me get just the right leverage. Then he used his thumb to rotate in circles over my clit, so that I got everything I wanted—the satisfaction of being filled and the necessary urging of his manual ministrations. I was momentarily completed by his large cock, and teased by his fingertips, and I felt as if I were flying when I came. Cindy's man came a moment later and then collapsed with spent pleasure, his eyes heavy, his breathing deep.

Once we were both finished, and I'd dressed myself

again, I did the ink job he wanted. I'm a professional, after all, and he was a paying customer. I'd gotten my closure from fucking him, somehow, and I felt pure inside and refreshed.

And maybe I spelled her name with an *S* instead of a *C*. He was too blindsided by postorgasmic bliss to check in the mirror to see.

So maybe I'm a little wicked, after all.

CCCCO

X-rated Wishes

⊰ BY ERIC WILLIAMS ⊱

HEN Matt caught the talking fish, he wasn't entirely surprised. He'd had far too many beers to be surprised by anything at this point. He simply stared at the wriggling trout in his hand—a fish that by all rights should have been changing colors, rapidly fading from its original iridescent glory to a flat, metal gray, but wasn't—and watched the gaping mouth part in an attempt to make him an offer he couldn't refuse.

"Let me go," the fish said in the deep, burbling voice of a CNN announcer, "and I'll grant you any wish."

Matt gazed at the trout, and then said in a drunken drawl, "*Any* wish?"

"You bet."

"Any wish," Matt repeated, mesmerized by the concept. "A million dollars. Or a fancy car. Or a better job. Or no job at all."

"Right on," the fish said.

Matt thought for a moment. "Just one wish?"

"No," the trout said, "you set me free and I'll grant you

any wish you want, whenever you come down to the stream and call out for me."

"Okay," Matt said, "in that case, I'd like you to make my wife want the type of sex I do." The beers had made him horny. For some reason, fishing out by himself always did make him ready for sex when he got home.

"And your type of sex is—?"

"You know," Matt shrugged. "A little back-door action."

"I understand where you're coming from," the fish said, "so try it tonight, after you sober up and shower off. Light some candles. Break out a big ol' bottle of the best sort of lube. Talk all sweet and sexy to her, and see what happens."

Matt tossed the fish back and then shook his head. "Never going to happen," he said out loud. Stella hadn't let him even touch that rosebud opening between her heart-shaped cheeks in months. What was the likelihood that he'd get to slide his rigid pole in there tonight? Still, it wasn't every day he met a talking fish, so he thought he'd just go ahead and follow the fish's suggestions and see what magic might occur. Who was he to doubt?

That night, he did exactly as the fish had told him, and he even went a little overboard, making the stunning red-headed Stella come twice on his tongue before sliding behind her and kissing all over her lovely round ass cheeks. How crazy, he'd always thought, that a woman with an ass made for fucking didn't like to engage in that sort of activity. "Dirty," she generally would say when he suggested it. "You know, Matt, I'm just not a dirty kind of girl."

Tonight was different. His wife wiggled, a little bit like the fish had in his hand, but she didn't say "no" or "stop" or anything. So Matt continued his movements, now parting her glorious ass cheeks and starting to kiss along the velvety alley between them. Usually, by this point, on the very few times he'd ever made it this far, she'd squirm away and cajole him into some other action. A blowjob. A hand-job. A doggy-style fuck, which was about as risqué as she ever got. Now, if he could believe his eyes, she was actually raising her hips up, arching to give him better access. She wanted him to go there! So Matt continued. He licked and skated his tongue around her opening, and then he parted her cheeks wide with his hands and breathed gently on her so that she could feel the warm tickle of air against her.

"Oh, fuck me," his wife begged. "Please fuck me—"

"Can I?" he asked, knowing she'd know what he meant.

"Jesus, yes. What are you waiting for?"

So he did. He slid his rock-hard cock into her tightest of openings, working slowly and steadily in case she changed her mind and wanted him to stop. But she didn't. To Matt's surprise and extreme delight, his wife cried out in pleasure. "Oh, god, Matt. Oh, god—"

Holding himself back when all he really wanted to do was pound into her, he pulled out slightly, then drizzled a fresh river of lube down over his cock. Then back he went inside of her, and he could feel her muscles tightening on him. She milked him. That's how into the action she was. Her body responded by tightening around his pole, and he thought he might scream, it felt so fucking good.

But somehow even in his heated state, he remembered the fish's advice, and he pulled out and poured more of the clear, sleek liquid down her split, and then slid back inside. She was loving it. He could tell. The way she moaned. The way she tossed her hair so that it fell like a ginger wave over her back. The way her eyelids fluttered and her full lips parted. Christ, she was loving every fucking second.

What a fish!

With one hand, he reached under her to play with her clit, and he found her as swollen and large as a hard candy. His fingertips only grazed against her, and that small touch was like pushing a magic button. As soon as he started to stroke her, his wife went wild. She started to moan louder and to milk his cock even harder, and before he even knew what was happening, Matt was coming deep inside of her ass. His fingers continued to work Stella's clit, and as he shot his load inside of her, Stella came with him, and now her muscles squeezed him even tighter, and he thought that nothing in his entire life had ever felt as good as that moment did. From the way her whole body seemed to glow with pleasure, it appeared as if Stella agreed with him.

"God, that was amazing," Stella murmured as the two untangled themselves. Matt sighed as he kissed her smooth, soft cheek, and then he remembered the fish had said he'd grant him any wish—whenever he went down to the river. But from the look on Stella's face he thought it might not be necessary anymore. And when she tossed one leg over his and said, "You know, baby, I've been wondering about a threesome. Me and Julia and you—"

Well, Matt knew that all of his X-rated wishes were about to be granted, for now and forever.

You Don't Know Me

❧ BY ISABELLE NATHE ❧

ELEEN was notoriously bad with names. She tried mnemonics. She tried parlor tricks of having two people whose names she was *supposed* to know already introduce each other rather than depend on her for assistance. She tried listening to mind-strengthening audiotapes while driving in her dashing red convertible during her morning commute. Finally, she simply started stating that she was notoriously bad with names and hope that nobody would be offended.

And then she met him.

It was at a cocktail party, one of those nightmare occasions for Deleen in which everyone said their names too damn fast for her to possibly catch on, and with the hearty rock-and-roll music playing and ambient conversation noise of happy partygoers, she had no fucking chance. If name tags would only gain in popularity as a fashion item, she'd be saved. But no such luck. Generally, she felt mildly depressed when she forgot someone's name. On this evening, she was mortified. Here was a man she could actually imagine going home with, one who she'd already imagined fucking up against the black-veined marble counter in the kitchen, and she couldn't for the life of her recall what his name was.

Luckily, he didn't seem to notice.

With a well-placed hand, he steered her to the master bedroom of the condo, then spread her out on the sumptuous black velvet bedcovers. As Deleen stared at him and watched him return the gaze, she found herself feeling pleased that she'd spent so long getting ready for the party. She knew she looked amazing, and she could tell that the man agreed with her silent assessment. Quietly, he busied himself undoing the tie at her hip and letting her deep crimson silk dress fall open, revealing her naked skin beneath.

"Deleen," he said, smiling down at her. "You're so fucking beautiful. I can't wait to be inside of you."

She looked up at him, desperate for him to make that statement come true, and she wished more than anything she could respond in kind. Wished she could say, "Oh, Liam." Or "Oh, Jacob." Or "Oh, Maxwell,"—anything other than what she did say, which was the rather pathetic: "Oh! Me too."

He had her feet up over his shoulders in moments and began sliding his long, hard cock deep into her. To her great satisfaction, he was as well endowed as she'd fantasized that he would be. Each thrust moved both her body and the bed, and Deleen started to sigh as she felt the glossy wetness of her own arousal spread beneath her. The man used his fingers to nuzzle apart her petal-soft pussy lips, and his firm thumbs danced knowingly over her clit in a rapid, delicate melody. First one, then the other, moved over her clit, tricking back and forth and making her even more slippery wet than she had been already. She knew that she was going to climax with him—*knew* it—and then he said, "When you come, say my name. I love it when a girl says my name at the very height of pleasure." His voice was hoarse with desire, and he gave her a slightly shy smile as he spoke, as if he'd revealed more secrets than he planned on sharing so soon. With a wave of sorrow, Deleen realized she'd have to tell him.

But no. Not yet. Because before she knew what he was doing, he pulled out, then flipped her easily over on the bed, so that he could get into her doggy-style. On her hands and knees, she glanced straight ahead into the oval-shaped gilded mirror over the king-size bed, and she thought in a wicked flash of amorous understanding that the hosts of the party must like to watch themselves when they fucked. That was something she'd never have dreamed about them in the past. They seemed so—well— uptight about things like that. But there was no reason to have a mirror here, unless it was for precisely this purpose: watching a carnal movie of one's own making. Few things were more arousing to Deleen, and she had a mirror in a similar spot in her own boudoir. One that she'd love to introduce to her brand-new man, if she could only remember his name.

Her new lover put one hand under her belly, and he moved his fingers languorously down to her pussy, running them up and down over her twitching clit until she suddenly—and surprisingly!—came on his fingertips. The strength of the climax left her panting, and as she worked to catch her breath, she looked into the mirror again and saw him shaking his head at her. Oh, she'd failed him. She saw the expression, knew precisely what it meant.

His hand, still sticky with her silky wet juices, came up high in the air and then landed like a thunderclap against her ass. "Bad girl," he said, his voice rich with mock disapproval, "I asked you for a simple request—"

"I'm sorry," she murmured, feeling despondent once again.

"I can give you so much pleasure," he promised her. "If you only return the favor. You don't know me," he continued, "but you can believe what I say. Especially, after a climax like that, can't you?" As he spoke, he continued to fuck her, moving in long, slow strokes that seemed to touch the very innermost parts of her body. She could feel herself heating up again, growing more aroused as the man continued to work her. He was going to make her cherry a second time in mere moments. When was the last time a lover had done that?

But what was his name?

She tried to relive the moment when they'd been introduced. Was it Ben? Or Miles? Or Sam? Was it something more exotic, a place name like York, or Paris, or Dallas? No, *those* names she would have remembered. Obscure monikers tended to stick with her more easily than simple ones. She was having such a difficult time thinking. He was getting in so deep now, and his hands roamed over her lovely lean body as he fucked her, tickling the indents at her waist, pulling open the cheeks of her ass so that he could peer between them.

This wasn't really like her—to fuck a stranger she'd just met at a party. Actually having sex *at* the party was even less like her. But he was so handsome, and so damn sexy, and she just hadn't been able to deny herself. Now, he was promising more pleasure, if she could fulfill his request and return the favor. But what the fuck was his name? What if she called out "Honey" or "Baby" or "Lover"? Would that work? She tilted her head and caught her own expression in the mirror, just before the man pulled out and flipped her over once again. Now, he moved over her body and then swiveled around into a sixty-nine. She parted her lips automatically and drew in the bulbous head of his cock, which was fragrantly anointed with her own sweet juices.

She'd always liked the sensation of going down on a man after he'd been inside her, but this time it was with both a combination of erotic heat and sweet relief that she started to suck him. With her mouth all full of his cock, he couldn't possibly expect her to say his name, could he? His full lips searched out the split of her body, and he went back and forth between suckling on her clit and bestowing soft, gentle kisses on the insides of her thighs. His thick dark hair tickled her skin when he moved his head, and she found that she was already cresting on the peak of a second orgasm. Her thoughts became filmy and light. She couldn't think to do anything but keep sucking on his rigid hard-on, until suddenly he pulled out, leaving her mouth empty and her heart fluttering.

"Please—" she said.

"I'll give it back to you if you say my name. I'll give you everything you want. Everything—"

To her total dismay, she realized that they were onto that game again. She couldn't do as he asked. Why was that so difficult to admit? She wanted to, that was for sure. She would have given anything to be able to say, "Jake," or "Joe," or "Bob," or "Johnny. Let me suck your big, hard cock. I'm begging you. Let me. I'm so hungry, I could swallow you whole. Swallow every last drop of yours."

It was as if he heard the thoughts in her head. "Anything?" he asked.

"What do you want?" she murmured, understanding that they had a connection. An unexplainable connection. And that she should simply move with it rather than put up a fight.

"Your ass," he said. "I want to be in your ass."

She nodded, feeling herself tightening and opening at the same time.

"Call my name out when I make you come on my tongue first," he instructed. "And then I'm going to slide around behind you, part those stunning rear cheeks of yours, and drive in deep. You're going to come again, Deleen, with my cock in your ass. I promise you that. And when you do, you call out my name, okay? Do that for me, baby?"

It was like a test between them. She didn't want to fail him. Not after he'd already made her come once, not with all the promised pleasure at stake. She simply nodded, and he went immediately back to licking her clit, using the whole of his tongue against her, until she was absolutely mewing with pleasure. He continued to lick and lap in great, looping circles until she came, and this time, she buried her face in her hands, hoping that he would think she had said his name, but that it was muffled in her moans and cries of pleasure.

Just as he'd promised, he moved quickly on the bed so that he was behind her, ready to enter her ass. He wet his fingertips and skated in circles around her hole, pressed just the tips inside of her to stretch the opening, and then his cock replaced his fingers and he began driving in deep. Deleen felt herself swooning against him. She was so relaxed from coming twice, and her body welcomed the man's cock with each thrust.

But as the excitement built within her once again, so did the fear at letting her lover down. How could she ever do what he asked? There was no way. No way at all, until the door suddenly swung open, and a man stared at them with harsh surprise on his face. Here was the host, out of place in his own bedroom, confused and conflicted. "Jesus, Michael," he groaned, an instant blush on his cheeks. And Deleen remembered it in a bright flash— Michael Rumsfield—a name that had been shortened he'd told her from "Rumpelstiltskin" by his grandfather when the man had arrived in America.

"Sorry, man—" the host said, and the door shut firmly behind him just as Michael reached his limits in Deleen's ass.

"Michael," she murmured as she came for a third—but not the final time—of the evening. "Oh, fuck, Michael," and he smiled as he wrapped one hand in her spun-gold mane of hair and primed her body for accepting each pleasure he had yet to offer.

CCCCO

Zoe White and the Seven Whores

BY THOMAS S. ROCHE

NCE upon a time in Lower Manhattan there were seven whores who worked in a clandestine high-class brothel located in a luxury suite on the forty-fourth floor. They saw a wide range of clients, all of whom had in common that they were exactly the same type of businessman. The seven whores were the best of friends, and as they started work just before lunch, they would happily sing in unison: "Hey, ho! Hey, ho! It's off to bed we go!" as they danced the cancan in their lingerie.

The madam of this brothel was an aging call girl who had become exceedingly bitter when her dreams of seducing a wealthy trick into marriage had not materialized. She had very little sense of aesthetics and as a result insisted on choosing each girl's professional name, which resulted in some very strange monikers for the poor little tarts.

The madam was very mean to the seven whores and insisted that every moment they spent in the brothel be turned to profit. She set up webcams in one of the bedrooms and demanded that while waiting for clients to show up the seven whores would perform lewd and unsavory sex acts with each other on camera. The madam routed these live feeds to a pay site that soon attracted many thousands of subscribers. The seven whores discovered, much to the madam's delight, that performing lewd and unsavory sex acts with each other between clients was vastly more fun than playing Parcheesi.

Soon the seven whores' frolicsome antics had attracted an international following of obsessed fans, especially after the madam hired a publicist and got them a media hit in *Adult Video News Online*. The seven whores so enjoyed their time together that some would show up several hours early for their shifts to cavort enthusiastically with each other on camera. The madam set up seven different Web pages for the seven different whores and made up all sorts of improbable biographical data about them ("Sexy first discovered her love of her own body when she was taken by the football team in the locker room after the big game," or "Kitschy is a humanities undergrad who always gets straight As without even turning in any of the class work—you do the math!" or "Nurse Kitty works at a local hospital and finds that her patients really appreciate the . . . *extra* TLC she gives them."

The seven whores didn't much care, however; anything that kept the webcam going was jake with them, since all they wanted to do was frolic, frolic, frolic, each mining the depths of her fellow whores' passion.

One day there came to the brothel a film student named Zoe White looking for a little extra cash, a cream-skinned beauty with long jet-black hair. She had figured out how to fit a surprising number of piercings into her breathtaking face, and she was covered head to toe with erotic tattoos, from the trysting Geishas on her back to the Gothic-scripted WHITE TRASH tattooed with little red bows across her thighs. Zoe White painted her lips bloodred and came fully equipped with her own improbable biography ("Zoe White haunts graveyards because she finds that the kind of man who hangs out there has that certain serial killer edge that really, really, *really* turns Zoe White on"). The madam immediately despised Zoe White and almost didn't hire her because, as she said, "My clients want a whore, not a pin-cushion, dearie."

But several of the brothel's clients had inquired of the madam if she had any employees who weren't quite the clean-scrubbed college girls with blonde hair and blue eyes that the madam exclusively hired. "I'll sic this weirdo on them," cackled the madam in private. "That'll show those slumming sons of bitches! See how they like *this* walk on the wild side."

The madam led Zoe White into the bedroom where the girls were cavorting on camera in a clusterfuck of collegiate style. The girls giggled and crowded around their new play-mate, and the madam introduced Zoe White to each of the seven whores.

"This is Sexy, Slutty, Kitschy, Cuddly, Horny, Submis-sive, and Nurse Kitty."

"Pleased to meet you," said Nurse Kitty, a rapturous blonde wearing cat ears and a skintight white latex nurse's outfit.

"Likewise," said Sexy, a bodacious vamp in a formfit-ting vintage red dress so low-cut Zoe White suspected it might have challenged a few laws of physics.

"So pleased to meet you," cooed Kitschy, a bottle-blonde

in pigtails and a schoolgirl's uniform, carrying a backpack with a familiar Japanese cat on it and a pair of sunglasses with an even more familiar mouse. Kitschy's eyes flickered up and down Zoe White's body in its sports bra, tight black bondage shorts, horizontal-striped stockings and knee-high combat boots.

"Nice piercings," said Slutty, tugging at the top her spandex minidress as one surgically enhanced breast popped out, the only result being that the other one popped out when the first popped in.

"We're so happy to have a new playmate," said Cuddly, embracing Zoe White and snuggling her face against her new friend's neck while she rubbed her tits against Zoe White's.

"Very good to meet you, mistress," said Submissive, a kneeling girl wearing nothing but a dog collar.

"Wanna fuck?" asked Horny.

"Yes, that's an interesting point," cackled the madam. "You see, Zoe White, if you're going to work in *my* brothel, you'll not only put out for the customers, but for your fellow whores on camera!!"

"Rock on!" said Zoe White, putting down her Addams Family lunchbox and producing a pair of matching dildos. She seized one in each hand and bum-rushed the king-size bed, which exploded into a soiree of sapphic exploration as the seven whores pounced on their fresh meat.

The madam stared in wonder as the seven whores welcomed Zoe White.

Over the next few weeks, clients flooded the madam with requests for the new girl's time. Unlike what the madam had expected, the polite Manhattan businessmen who had previously been satisfied with the pristine bodies of the seven whores were now fascinated by the pierced and tattooed Zoe White, one guy even mortgaging his Jersey Shore house to see her more often. What's more, Zoe White was the best lay in the place, something each of the seven whores would cheerfully concede since they'd all enjoyed the new girl's talents, thrilled by her spontaneous real orgasms, adventurous nature, and charming personality. Word of Zoe White spread like wildfire, and soon the madam had to schedule appointments with her around the clock. Zoe White never seemed to get tired, though, becoming only more and more enthusiastic with each client as she serviced a long line of them snaking around the block—or perhaps it would be more accurate to say that they serviced *her*. Or attempted to.

The seven whores were dismayed, because now their playmate was not as available for their between-client antics. But so fond were their feelings for Zoe White that they begged to do doubles with her, and the madam soon started a two-for-one deal on alternate Tuesdays. The seven whores and Zoe White were very happy. And their clients were absolutely fucking thrilled.

Despite the steady rise in income, the madam grew more and more bitter toward Zoe White, muttering to herself, "What's that pincushion got that I haven't got?" as she posed herself in the mirror wearing the lingerie that had adorned her body when she'd been a successful whore and not the hagged-out slut she was nowadays. She started programming pop-up windows into Zoe White's page on the brothel's Web site, flashing messages like "Come visit Zoe White! She only has six or seven communicable diseases!" When the seven whores noticed and inquired about these pop-up windows (Zoe White was entirely too busy with clients to ever bother to check out her own Web page), the madam feigned the innocent, doe-eyed look that had served her so well in her earlier days, and said with a sigh, "Those darn hacker kids! I'll e-mail our service provider and ask them if there's any way to improve security on the site. I'll get back to you in a few weeks!"

But no matter what the bitter madam did, Zoe White only became more popular. Men came from all over the world to frolic with the raven-haired and silver-pierced beauty.

The bitter madam came up with a plan.

She started a contest on the site:

WHO'S THE FAIREST OF THEM ALL?
VOTE FOR YOUR FAVORITE WHORE AND
ENTER A RAFFLE TO WIN A NIGHT WITH HER

The madam snapped digital photographs of the girls, making sure to shoot Zoe White from the most unflattering angle possible.

Into the thumbnails of the seven whores and Zoe White, she slipped a picture of herself at the height of her powers. She really was quite a fetching young thing, her voluptuous body decked out in a red garter belt and push-up bra. The seven whores all wondered who this sexy woman on their Web site was, but the madam refused to tell them. In any event, the contest started with a spam campaign going out to 15 billion e-mail addresses world-wide. Soon the votes were racking up, and in dismay the bitter madam watched as Zoe White received first a zillion votes, then two zillion, and finally a zillion zillion. Despite her unconventional appearance, Zoe White was clearly the fairest of them all, the seven whores receiving respectable showings but coming nowhere near the zillion zillion votes that Zoe White received. One guy in Ohio voted for the bitter madam, which only added insult to injury.

The bitter old madam swore to find a way to bring Zoe White down—she would exhaust the poor girl with an endless line of men.

"Oh, look," she told Zoe White. "Now that we've held the drawing for the winning whore, it turns out we have a zillion zillion winners. Guess you'll just have to fuck all of them, you little bitch!"

Far from protesting, Zoe White shrugged and trotted into the bedroom, opening up her Munsters backpack and taking out a bottle of almond oil, enlisting the aid of the seven whores to slick herself up for the oncoming clients.

The madam contacted all the contest participants by e-mail, inviting them to the Zoe White gang bang on Memorial Day weekend—on the house. Entranced by Zoe White's beauty, the contest participants came from all over, some hitchhiking, some hopping freight trains, others flying in on private jets. Zoe White sprawled out in the bedroom and eagerly serviced each of the men in turn. The line went out Zoe White's bedroom, out the door of the brothel, up and then down the stairs of the forty-four-story building, out the door, around the block, across the harbor and right up the Statue of Liberty's stairs to the very top of her torch.

"At long last!" cackled the madam. "That little pincushion's had it!"

But to the madam's dismay, Zoe White's enthusiasm

proved boundless. The madam watched as she made her
way through the line with aplomb, sending each of her
clients away satisfied and exhausted. Zoe White's skills and
enthusiasm were shocking, and the madam watched in
horror as the enraptured girl swirled her tongue around the
engorged apple-red head of each man's cock and tonguing
his ripe balls before begging him to fuck her. The seven
whores set up folding chairs next to Zoe White's bed and
cheered her on, saying, "You show 'em, Zoey!"

When all zillion zillion of the contest participants had
been tidily taken care of by Zoe White, the poor girl fell
into an exhausted slumber on her well-used bed, snoring
cheerfully.

"No!" shrieked the bitter madam, her face turning red
as she jumped up and down and screamed. "It's not possible! The bitch must die!"

"Jesus, you look like you could use a tongue job," said
Slutty and Horny in unison, and giggled as they turned toward each other and tittered, "Jinx!"

They trundled the struggling madam onto Zoe White's
bed and held her down as they began to service her with
their eager mouths, having become quite aroused from
watching Zoe White's long ordeal. As the madam thrashed
on the bed under the two whores, Zoe White found herself
sleepily awakening and, thinking she was still in the middle of the Zoe White Memorial Day gang bang, climbed
onto the madam and began to make love to her. Horny and
Slutty were a tad disappointed, but they backed off and left
it to the master. At first the madam protested, but soon under the ministrations of Zoe White's unbelievably skilled
and enthusiastic mouth, she was cooing and moaning in
orgasm.

When the madam had been brought to orgasm more times than she could count by Zoe White, the younger girl cuddled up next to the madam and recognized her for the first time.

"Oh, my," sighed the madam. "I think I love you, Zoe White!"

"Then why are you always such a bitch to me?" asked Zoe White. "I know you wrote those things on my Web page!"

"I think I was jealous," said the madam. "You girls are all so young and beautiful, and you're so exotic! I used to be a pretty whore."

"You're still pretty!" said Zoe White. "You're just kind of a raging pain in the ass!"

"I don't mean to be," said the madam. "Well, actually, that's a lie. I'm a pain in the ass because I'm mad you girls are so much prettier than me."

"But you *are* pretty! You're beautiful, in fact! And you can be as exotic as you want to be!"

"But I could never be a whore," sobbed the madam. "Not as old as I am!"

"Bull fucking shit!" said Zoe White, slapping the madam playfully on one ample tit. "Do you have any idea how many guys fantasize about hot, dominant older women showing them the ropes? I mean, you've got the experience, right? You know a lot more about sex than me or the other girls!"

"Really?"

"Really! I bet with the right Web designer you could do a brisk trade in men—especially younger men!"

The madam's eyes widened. "*Younger* men?"

"Yes!" Zoe White narrowed her eyes and stepped back,

lifting her hands into the sort of frame that pretentious film students use when evaluating a scene. "I could see you as the kinky older aunt fantasy. Guys will love you!"

With that, the madam agreed to visit Zoe White's piercing parlor in the East Village the next afternoon and have her pussy adorned with the sexy silver rings Zoe White favored. The seven whores gave the madam a makeover and dressed her up in sexy lingerie, helping her to design a Web page with digital photographs that showed her to great advantage. Soon the madam had developed her own following, and the seven whores had given her a new professional name: Princess Charming.

The seven whores and Zoe White and Princess Charming all worked together in the brothel, none of them wanting for well-paying clients. Princess Charming became one of the members' favorite performers, discovering now that she'd stopped being such a bitch that her enthusiasm for sex and vast wealth of experience made her even more fun to watch than the frolicsome Sexy, Slutty, Kitschy, Cuddly, Horny, Submissive, and Nurse Kitty, each of whom had her own devoted following.

With the money she made at the brothel, Zoe White finished her film degree and made a documentary film, calling it: *Princess Charming: Portrait of a 21st-Century Feminist Sexual Icon*. It received high marks at an independent film festival, and Zoe White is currently negotiating with several video companies to make a big-budget all-girl erotic feature starring Princess Charming and the seven whores. Zoe White retained a literary agent from her extensive list of satisfied clients and sold her memoirs to a major publisher for a mid-seven-figure advance. The seven whores and Princess Charming frolicked together on webcam while Zoe White traveled around the world giving lectures on women's sexual empowerment as a springboard for socio-cultural radicalism, and frolicking with former clients in each city she visited.

And they lived happily ever after.

ABOUT THOSE NAUGHTY AUTHORS

Xavier Acton ("Jo White and Cocksucker Red") has written for Web sites including Gothic.net, GoodVibes.com, and 13thStreet.com as well as the bestselling anthology *Sweet Life* (Cleis).

Ann Blakely ("Once Upon a Time") is the coauthor of *The Other Rules: Never Wear Panties on a First Date and Other Tips*. This spoof of the dating guide *The Rules* was recently translated into Spanish. Ms. Blakely lives in Manhattan. Her short stories have also appeared in *Sweet Life* I & II (Cleis), in *Naughty Stories from A to Z*, Volumes 1 & 2 (PTP), and on the Web site www.good vibes.com.

M. Christian ("Bells on Her Toes") has written stories that have appeared in *Best American Erotica, Best Gay Erotica, Best Lesbian Erotica, Best Transgendered Erotica, Friction*, and more than 150 other anthologies, magazines, and Web sites. He's the editor of more than twelve anthologies, including *Best S/M Erotica, Love Under Foot* (with Greg Wharton), *Underground* (with Paul Willis), *The Burning*

Pen, Guilty Pleasures, and many others. He's the author of three collections, the Lambda-nominated *Dirty Words* (gay erotica), *Speaking Parts* (lesbian erotica), and *The Bachelor Machine* (science-fiction erotica).

Dante Davidson ("Mistress, to You") is the pseudonym of a professor who teaches in Santa Barbara, California. His short stories have appeared in *Bondage* (Masquerade), *Naughty Stories from A to Z*, Volumes I & II (PTP), and *Sweet Life* I and II (Cleis). With Alison Tyler, he is the coauthor of the bestselling collection of short fiction *Bondage on a Budget* (PTP) and *Secrets for Great Sex After Fifty* (Poundridge), which he wrote at age twenty-eight.

Andre Farmer ("A Very Golden Goosing") is an aspiring literary writer who enjoys penning naughty tales for his lovers. This is his first published story.

Carole Few ("Queuing Up") has written for a variety of underground-style 'zines. Her work has appeared in *Come Quickly for Girls on the Go* (Rosebud), *Naughty Stories from A to Z* (PTP), and under pseudonyms on Web sites including www.cleansheets.com, www.tinynibbles.com, and www.worth.com. She is a college dropout but considers herself fully schooled in life.

Florence Hoard ("Earthly Delights") is obsessed with the piano. When she isn't playing, her fingers need something to do, so she writes. She creates music and fiction in San Francisco.

K.C. ("If the Stiletto Fits") is the pseudonym of a well-known erotic writer who believes some things are just a little too naughty even for the usual pseudonym. K.C.'s writing has appeared in *Sweet Life II: Erotic Fantasies for Couples* (Cleis).

Ronald Keller ("The Princess and the Penis") is a Web nerd who really, really loves sleepy women. He keeps his apartment stocked with hot cocoa, Enya CDs, and big, fluffy pillows.

Molly Laster ("For Want of a Nail") has written stories for *Naughty Stories from A to Z*, Volumes 1 & 2 (PTP), and the Web site www.goodvibes.com.

G. Lipton ("Lucky Number Seven") is a freelance photographer and amateur videographer living in Chicago. If he were one of the seven dwarfs, he would be Horny.

Cherie McIntosh ("Never Talk to Strangers") is a casting assistant in Los Angeles trying to break in as an actress. She has worked on many films, including the Billy Crystal feature *Mr. Saturday Night*, and she wishes she didn't have to say no quite so often.

Julia Moore ("King's Counting House") is the coauthor of the bestselling book *The Other Rules: Never Wear Panties on a First Date and Other Tips* (Masquerade), a spoof of the tragic dating guide *The Rules*. Her short stories have appeared in *Sweet Life* I & II (Cleis), *Naughty Stories from A to Z* (PTP), *Batteries Not Included* (Diva), and on the Web site www.goodvibes.com.

Tyler Morgan ("Clever Jack") has written for anthologies including *Naughty Stories from A to Z*, Volume 2 (PTP). Raised in Texas, Mr. Morgan now splits his time between London and Manhattan.

Isabelle Nathe ("You Don't Know Me") has written for anthologies, including *Come Quickly for Girls on the Go* (Rosebud), and *A Century of Lesbian Erotica* (Masquerade). Her work has appeared on the Web site www.goodvibes.com and in the anthology *Naughty Stories from A to Z* (PTP).

Jesse Nelson ("Undressed") lives with his girlfriend in Santa Monica where he spends too much time surfing and not enough time working. His short stories have appeared in *Sweet Life* II (Cleis). He dedicates this story to Hailey.

Emilie Paris ("Stealing Hearts") is a writer and editor. Her first novel *Valentine* (Blue Moon) is available on audiotape by Passion Press. She abridged the seventeenth-century novel *The Carnal Prayer Mat* for Passion Press. The audiotape won a *Publishers Weekly* best audio award in the "Sexcapades" category. Her short stories have also appeared in *Naughty Stories from A to Z*, Volumes I & II (PTP) and in *Sweet Life* I & II (Cleis) and on the Web site www.goodvibes.com.

Melody Perry ("Raver Ali and the Glo-Stick") is a Marin County dance instructor who dabbles in erotic writing. Her work has appeared in the anthologies *MASTER* and *slave,* edited by N. T. Morley, as well as several smaller 'zines and Web sites.

Thomas S. Roche ("Zoe White and the Seven Whores") is the author of more than two hundred published short stories that have appeared in a wide variety of magazines, Web sites, and anthologies including the *Best American Erotica* series. His most recent books are *His* and *Hers*, two books of erotica cowritten with Alison Tyler. After six years in the advertising industry and five as a full-time writer and editor, he is currently the marketing manager at San Francisco's Good Vibrations.

Erin Sanders ("Hannah & Greta") is a Midwestern submissive who has recently taken up comedy writing. She resides with her longtime partner near St. Louis, Missouri.

Echo Thomas ("Goldicocks and the Three Pairs") is a world traveler with a fetish for porridge. "Goldicocks" is Echo's first published story.

Alison Tyler ("All McQueen's Men") is undeniably a naughty girl. With best friend Dante Davidson, she is the coeditor of the bestselling collection of short stories *Bondage on a Budget* (PTP). Her short stories have appeared in anthologies including *Sweet Life* I & II (Cleis), *Wicked Words* 4, 5, 6, & 8 (Black Lace), *Best Women's Erotica* 2002 & 2003 (Cleis), *Guilty Pleasures* (Black Books), and *Sex Toy Tales* (Down There Press). She is the author of more than fifteen novels, including *Learning to Love It, Strictly Confidential, Sweet Thing, Sticky Fingers,* and *Something About Workmen* (all published by Black Lace), and *The ESP Affair* and *Blue Valentine* (published by Magic

Carpet). Ms. Tyler lives in the San Francisco Bay Area, but she misses L.A.

Mia Underwood ("Ducks to Swans") lives and works in the Fairfax region of Los Angeles. She enjoyed her tenth high-school reunion immensely and looks forward with happy anticipation to her fifteenth. Go Vikings!

Sage Vivant ("The Trials of Lady Vicarious") is the proprietress of Custom Erotica Source (www.customerotica source.com), where she and a small cadre of writers have been creating tailor-made erotic fiction for individual clients since 1998. She has been a guest on numerous television and radio shows nationwide, where she reads stories written for the hosts. Her work has appeared on various Web sites and been published in *Maxim, Forum UK*, and *Erotica* magazines. Several of her short stories appear in anthologies published in 2003.

Mila Whitely ("Wicked Sisters") has written for *Naughty Stories from A to Z*, Volume 2 (PTP) and *Girls on the Go* (Masquerade). She's currently saving up for her sixth tattoo, but she's not going to tell you where it will be.

Eric Williams ("X-rated Wishes") has written for anthologies, including *Sweet Life* (Cleis) and *Naughty Stories from A to Z* (PTP). He is an avid fisherman who firmly believes in happily ever after.

BONUS CHAPTER!

A Final Fairy Tale

❧ BY BETTINA NELSON ❧

HEN I was little, I was a princess every Halloween. My progressive parents tried to persuade me to be something more original. A beatnik. Martha Washington. A cowgirl. They couldn't stand that I was so entwined in a feminine fantasy. But I balked at their suggestions. Every October 31, I wrapped a silver scarf around myself, raided my mom's jewelry and makeup, and transformed myself into a creature of angelic beauty—or so I thought. (Pictures reveal that I drew huge rosy circles of rouge on my cheeks and tottered about in glittering heels much too big for my small feet.)

As an adult, I find myself each Halloween searching for something funky to wear to our office party. I work for a weekly paper, and we rent an entire restaurant for our festivities. Most of my coworkers are extremely creative. In the past, they have come dressed as refrigerators, as pairs of running shoes, as fried eggs with toast. But each Halloween, as I paw through my closet of black suits, I long for a silver scarf, some tall heels, and a rouge stick. The princess craving has never left.

When Joy and I hooked up, I could tell that she thought of me as strictly a businesswoman. I am that way on a day-to-day basis. My job as page editor of the drama section is fun but difficult. Invariably some story will arrive last minute. No matter how far we plan ahead, some picture is always late. I had more freedom when I wrote stories and didn't edit. Now, it's my ass if a deadline isn't made.

Joy seemed fine with my no-nonsense personality. She is a costume designer for movies, and her job allows her to constantly express her creativity. But on our first Halloween as a couple, I surprised her, confessing to her my desire to be a princess.

To my immediately relief, she didn't laugh at me. She didn't snicker as she looked up and down my nearly six-foot-tall body, didn't point out that I'm taller than your average prince, that I don't have any of the soft, feminine qualities held by princesses in fairy tales. Instead, she said, "No problem. Leave everything up to me."

On Halloween, in the late afternoon, she drove to my house with a huge garment bag. The first thing she did was blindfold me. Then, as I questioned and quizzed, she dressed me. She took the blindfold off to do my hair and makeup, but forced me to close my eyes until the last possible moment, allowing me to open them only because she needed to brush on coats of mascara. I trembled inside, wondering what transformation was taking place without my knowledge, or my full consent.

When she brought me to the mirror, I was in shock. She had dressed me in a silver shimmering outfit, made of the same gauzy, semi-sheer material of my mother's scarf. Joy had found a dress that suited my flat chest and long torso, and I appeared as light and feminine as I ever had in my dreams. She'd done my hair in ringlets and they fell loosely down my back. From my little crown to my sparkling shoes, I was a princess.

Joy left me alone while she dressed. Then came the second surprise of the evening: Joy dressed in the white breeches and velvet jacket of Prince Charming, and as such a couple, we made our way to the office party. Most of my coworkers didn't recognize me out of my normal business-suit attire. Once the thrill of surprise was over, Joy and I made our way to the roof, where we enacted another one of my fantasies, that of the princess giving up her maiden-head to the prince.

Joy, who acts in the role of the receiver during much of our lovemaking, was transcendent in her new role. She unfurled her cape and spread it out on the ground to protect me. Then, with me in my finery on the silken lining of her cape, she unsheathed her sword (so to speak) and plundered away. I was careful not to rip the lovely costume, lifting it up for her to gain access. That was the last coherent thought I had, though, because being taken by so handsome a prince left me dizzy and somewhat confused.

Joy cradled my head in her hands as she plunged her cock inside me. She cooed love words at me, calling me her precious gem, her most treasured prize, saying that she'd slay a dragon to capture my heart . . . but slaying me more with her tool, parting my private hedges and plunging inside for the treasure.

I cried out as she found the rollicking rhythm I like best, the beating of her hips like the beating of my heart, pounding, pounding. Her feverish kisses smeared my lipstick, but I didn't care. Her rough caresses, pawing at the bodice of my breasts, undid the laces, setting my small breasts free for her to kiss. She ravaged my breasts, nipping at them, biting them until I was writhing under her and begging for her to make me come.

That sped her up until she was rocking in and out of my cunt like a wild stallion, using her arms for leverage, gaining momentum with each stroke. I screamed as I came, though my voice was lost into the night, and I'm sure I didn't scare too many of the trick-or-treaters down below.

When I regained my sensibilities, Prince Charming was above me with his hand out to me, reaching to help me stand. He steadied me, then shook off his velvet cloak and wrapped it around his most muscular form. As he led me back into the party, he whispered, in a voice so similar to my lovely Joy, "And they lived happily ever after."

The End